The Amish Mail-Order Groom

He was here because of her *fater*'s woodworking—*nee* other reason. *As I told my* bruder . . . *she's incidental and only that.* Still, it was difficult to dismiss her beauty, and he watched her perfectly formed lips closely as she prepared to speak.

"According to tradition, a mail-order groom . . . is prepared to marry upon arrival and the meeting of his bride." She lowered her voice. "Now, tell me, do you find me adequate, Herr King?"

Her question sent a rush of warmth down his spine, but he answered with a coolness he didn't feel. "Surely, but there is always more to beauty than the exterior, Tabitha. Like a pine veneer that hides a wealth of burled elm, true beauty lies within."

"That's not what most men think," she muttered.

MARRYING MATTHEW

The Amish Mail Order Grooms

KELLY LONG

ZEBRA BOOKS
KENSINGTON PUBLISHING CORP.
www.kensingtonbooks.com

To Grant Long for Remembering Blackberry Falls

ZEBRA BOOKS are published by

Kensington Publishing Corp.
119 West 40th Street
New York, NY 10018

All Kensington titles, imprints, and distributed lines are available at special quantity discounts for bulk purchases for sales promotion, premiums, fund-raising, educational, or institutional use.

Special book excerpts or customized printings can also be created to fit specific needs. For details, write or phone the office of the Kensington Sales Manager: Attn.: Sales Department. Kensington Publishing Corp., 119 West 40th Street, New York, NY 10018. Phone: 1-800-221-2647.

Zebra and the Z logo Reg. U.S. Pat. & TM Off.
BOUQUET Reg. U.S. Pat. & TM Off.

First Printing: December 2020
ISBN-13: 978-1-4201-5165-7
ISBN-10: 1-4201-5165-7

ISBN-13: 978-1-4201-5166-4 (eBook)
ISBN-10: 1-4201-5166-5 (eBook)

10 9 8 7 6 5 4 3 2 1

Printed in the United States of America

Prologue

Blackberry Falls, PA

WANTED: An Amish Mail-Order Groom. Age 20–35. Must be willing to live in remote Appalachia and build life in said community. Must love books, horses, and possess good teeth. Appearance must be tolerable at least, though bride would favor a *gut* mind over looks. Must understand a woman's sensibilities and not be judgmental. Must realize that *Gott* is the Third in a marriage. Reply to . . .

Twenty-year-old Tabitha Stolfus knew that she was both the sole heir of her *fater*'s company and his sole lament.

"If only you'd been born a *buwe*," he'd wail at times. "Or if only you'd marry! Why can't you marry, Tabby? And why must you be so headstrong?"

Tabitha had heard the words so often, she could almost put them to song. But she had finally had enough and had taken out an ad in the *Renova Record*, a small

Englisch and *Amisch* newspaper far from her home in the Allegheny Mountains.

If I'm to have a husband, she'd considered, *let it be some man who isn't so familiar with what wealth Stolfus Lumber and Woodworking means. Then I will make sure he meets the qualifications that I lay out—not my* fater*'s.*

The idea she'd whispered to herself took root in her mind and grew, and soon a detailed ad was submitted to the far-off *Record*. And, to her surprise, because she'd never actually heard of a mail-order groom, an *Amisch* man responded. . . . Rather coolly, she thought, but nonetheless a response. . . .

She'd kept the letter in the bosom of her shift beneath her carefully pinned collar, and she occasionally slid out the paper to read, trying hard to spot anything suspicious that might lie within the words. But even she had to admit that Matthew King sounded much to her liking. He didn't seem to know about Stolfus Lumber and Woodworking and he didn't seem to possess the self-interest common to some of the local men who'd tried to win her hand . . . and her purse. *Jah*, Matthew King would do just fine. . . .

"Have you lost your mind, big *bruder*?"

Matthew King shot his younger sibling, Caleb, a wry glance, then resumed packing. "I've told you—her da runs one of the best woodworking outfits in the mountains."

Caleb snorted. "Then *geh* and ask to apprentice with him. You don't need to do something *narrisch* like marrying his headstrong *dochder*. I've heard she's as wild as a colt and not exactly marriage material."

"It doesn't matter. I'm sick of pounding out the most basic of furniture. I want to learn what only her *fater* can teach—the art and craftsmanship of woodworking. And Herr Stolfus doesn't favor taking on apprentices. Marrying the girl is incidental. . . ."

As pouring rain thrummed on his back and dripped from the brim of his hat, Matthew recalled the words he'd spoken to his *bruder* with a faint lift of his lips. Then he swiped his arm across his wet face for about the tenth time that morning. It had been raining steadily since he'd left home three days before as he and his hulking guide made their way deep into the Allegheny Mountains, the foothills of Appalachia. During their trek, Matthew had wondered idly if Blackberry Falls was simply a myth. However, there was nothing mythlike about the big-framed *Amisch* man who was leading him. Abner, as he'd introduced himself with a massive paw of a hand, spoke simply.

"I'm Abner Mast. Right-hand man of Herr Stolfus and his *dochder*'s guardian. I've been responsible for ensuring her safety since she was but a child."

Matthew nodded, sensing that there was a test somewhere in the *aulder* man's words, so he kept silent.

Abner grunted after a moment, then growled over the cadence of the rain. "I don't hold with what the maid is doing, marrying blind, and an outsider at that. But I guard her secrets well, so keep that in yer head, *buwe*, for I'll not see her harmed in any way."

Matthew realized that it would be of little use to say that he'd never harmed a woman. He could only imagine what rabbit trails such a comment would produce in *auld* Abner's mind, so once more, he remained quiet.

"Ya don't have much to say fer yerself, *buwe*. Nothing wrong with a man keeping his own counsel—I'll give ya that—but still water runs deep, and Blackberry Falls will not easily welcome a stranger, no matter who he's *kumme* to marry."

"*Danki*," Matthew said lightly; then he was distracted by a stand of virgin sugar maple near the muddy trail. He put out a hand and touched the bark of the nearest tree with something akin to a caress.

Abner grunted in obviously reluctant approval. "Well, ya touch that tree like ya would a woman, so perhaps ya ain't so strange."

Matthew smiled, unconcerned by the other man's dire attitude. *Here was virgin timber, and there would be men who knew how best to work it.* Any thought of Tabitha Stolfus drifted from his mind as he turned his face upward into the rain and thanked *Gott* for bringing him to Blackberry Falls. . . .

Chapter One

"*Nee*, bring me the yellow." Tabitha Stolfus frowned slightly as she gazed into the large, cherrywood-framed mirror in her bedroom. She knew that having such a big mirror might be considered vanity, but she had a good reason for possessing it.

She stood in a light shift, having discarded the blue dress that her faithful housemaid, Anke, had first brought her.

"Yellow?" the *aulder* woman said in a severe but hushed tone. "Ye're not to wear anything but blue to be married. And ya know that . . . Why, if yer *fater* finds out, he'll have a fit."

"As you know, my *fater* is deep in the high timber, looking for red oak. He's not due back until tomorrow, and by then, it'll all be over with." Tabitha took a graceful step away from the mirror and lightly skimmed her trim waistline with her slender hands. Her honey-blond hair hung below her hips in graceful waves and she knew, without conceit, that her face was as comely as her form.

Anke handed her the other dress, yellow as freshly churned butter. "*Jah*, all over with—and you'll be hitched to an *Amischer* ya know nothing about. And just suppose this man doesn't take to marryin' straightaway? Suppose he wants time ta get to know ya? Huh?"

Tabitha slipped on the pretty dress, then eased it over her hips. She stared into the mirror, her sapphire-blue eyes set with determination. "The man is a mail-order groom, Anke. He surely must know that if the roles were reversed, a mail-order bride would be expected to marry upon her arrival."

"Humph, well, I still say it ain't a healthy idea ta marry without knowin' each other. And what will ya do if you suddenly fall in love—true love—with some other fella, but yer forever bound to—what's his name again?"

"Matthew," Tabitha said firmly. "I'm marrying Matthew King, on my own terms, by my own judgment. All will be well. You'll see, Anke. Now, *sei se gut*, help me with my hair and *kapp*; I'm going to *geh* out for a quick walk to clear my mind before I'm due to meet Abner . . . and Matthew . . . in the big clearing."

Anke approached with a light comb, still muttering, and Tabitha caught the *auld* woman's hand and pulled her close for a quick squeeze. "*Danki* for loving me, Anke, and please stop worrying. Things have a way of working out."

"*Jah*, some might say that, *kind*, but you should know better. It's *Gott* Who works things out, and He sometimes sees things a mite different from us."

Tabitha merely smiled in response, certain in her heart that she was acting in accordance with *Gott*'s plans. . . .

Matthew realized that their trek was nearing its end when Abner lowered his bulging knapsack to the ground near a bubbling stream and pool of water.

"Yer filthy and ya smell," Abner said in gloomy tones.

"*Danki*," Matthew returned. "I could remark that you look like a muddy toad, but that wouldn't be quite right, now would it? Not when the thought of soggy vermin might be more the thing."

"Watch yer mouth, *buwe*. . . . She wouldn't want ta see ya lookin' such a mess, so ye'd best git ta bathing."

Matthew needed no further invitation. Turning his back to Abner, he quickly lowered his suspenders, then worked the hook-and-eye closures on his muddy, once-white shirt.

"You need pins," Abner said.

Matthew half turned, his shirt in his hand. "Pins?"

"We use pins here to fasten our clothing."

"That must be painful at times." He undid the waistband of his black pants, then raised an eyebrow at Abner. "I forgot my straight razor. I don't suppose you would . . ."

Abner rooted out a brutal-looking knife from his satchel and tossed it to him.

"Thanks," Matthew said drily as he finished undressing, then plunged into the icy-cold water of the creek's swimming hole. From the creek bank, Abner threw him a rough bar of soap.

"I'd best *geh* and find the *maedel*. You hurry on."

"*Jah*. Got it." Matthew lathered his arms and watched Abner slip away into the forest. It was *gut* to simply draw a deep breath and relax into the cold waters. He stared up at the canopy of green tree branches and began to lather his face. Then he plied the knife against his jaw; the edge could have proven hazardous had he not known well how to manage a blade. He was washing his hair when an abrupt sound caused him to look up at the bank.

"This is private land. What are you doing here?"

Matthew lowered his hands and blinked at the vision of loveliness his inquisitor presented. Honey-gold hair escaped her prayer *kapp* and curled in enticing tendrils against her fair cheeks. Her feminine shape was emphasized by the pristine apron she wore over a butter-yellow dress, and her stance, although she was petite, was one of strength. He knew instinctively, as surely as if she'd shouted her name to him, that this was Tabitha Stolfus—his *frau*-to-be.

He cleared his throat. "I'm bathing, but I don't want to offend your maidenly . . . sensibilities with such an admission." He ran his hands through his soapy hair and pulled until he knew he must surely look like a pointy-headed *narrisch* man.

He watched her pink lips turn down into a slight frown. "My sensibilities are hardly offended, sir, and I doubt you'd cause me much trouble anyway."

"Well—" He splashed at the water in front of him and feigned rising to his feet. "In that case . . ."

He expected her to at least turn away, but she stood her ground until he ducked under the water and hastily rinsed his hair.

Sensibilities . . . Tabitha resisted the urge to take out the letter hidden in her bodice and study it once more, but then she was distracted by the sudden thrumming of her pulse. The stranger was like some big cat, lazily playing in the icy water while she tried to understand why something about him seemed oddly familiar.

She watched as he reemerged from beneath the soap

bubbles on the surface of the water and shook his dark head. His shoulders were broad and his chest finely muscled. And she couldn't resist a hasty glance downward to where dark hair arrowed from his belly into the swirl of the water.

She straightened her shoulders, then snapped her attention back to the situation at hand. "I suggest you make yourself scarce when you've finished your . . . bathing."

"*Danki* for the advice. I'll think on it."

She nodded, then turned away to continue her walk. But her peace of mind had been shaken by the ruffian in the creek. . . .

Abner sighed to himself as he lengthened his strides along the wooded path. His back ached a bit from the recent journey and he felt every one of his forty-seven years. *Not* auld . . . *not yet* . . . He let the truth of his words quicken his steps as his heart gained momentum. He had every intention of seeking out Tabitha, but first he wanted the chance to lay eyes on Anke. He let his mind drift to thoughts of her pleasantly rounded shape, and the way her face flushed with heat when she was working at the laundry outside or canning corn at the cookstove. He longed to be able to help her with her work but knew she was proud and wouldn't appreciate a man interfering—especially the right hand of Herr Stolfus. In truth, he was John Stolfus's half *bruder*, but few knew this *auld*, well-kept secret. He'd been born on the wrong side of the quilt, of an unwanted pregnancy, with no *fater* to help him grow. Still, in the deep backwoods of the Alleghenies, he'd survived to manhood, used to running wild until

John had *kumme* for him and offered him a place, a job, a home.

Now he hurried his steps, knowing he was late meeting Tabitha in the big clearing. But because he understood the kind, he wasn't too concerned; he knew she was still probably fussing with her dress. He rounded a corner of the trail, then looked up, amazed as always at the workmanship displayed in the Stolfus *haus*. Truly more than a mere cabin, it rose to three stories, with windows framed by hauled stone from the creek. Abner knew that John Stolfus believed the *Amisch* adage that there is no beauty without purpose, and the purpose of his home was to be a place dedicated to Gott, to offer a location for the *Amisch* of Blackberry Falls to gather together in comfort and in times of trouble And besides, that *narrisch* Bishop Kore had approved the *haus* even though it was much bigger than the small cabins of the other *Amisch*.

Abner mounted the wide, wooden steps and then gave a thundering knock on the heavy wood of the front door. He heard oncoming steps from the other side and whipped off his black hat, hastily running his hand through his thick, graying-blond hair.

Anke opened the door and he smiled down at her. She was obviously busy and gave him a slightly vexed glare as she jerked her apron into tidiness.

"Ye're back, then, with the *buwe?*" she half whispered.

"*Jah*. Is she ready?" He had to resist the urge to reach out and touch one of the brown curls that had slipped the rigorous confines of Anke's work kerchief.

"She's already off to meet ya. She said she wanted ta walk a bit before she went to the clearing."

Abner swallowed hard and nodded. It would be so easy

to bend down and press his mouth to the red of her lips. But . . . his duty waited. "*Danki*." He slipped his hat back on and returned to the steps, walking away without looking back.

Anke watched Abner's broad back as he descended the steps. The man was a giant—plain and simple. She always felt small and delicate around him, even though she knew that her belly and bosom were far too big. But she also knew that she should not be thinking of Abner, not when she could remember all too clearly the horrid touch of her *oncle* when she was ten years *auld*. . . . She sighed to herself as she gently closed the heavy door and laid aside all personal thoughts to go to prepare a bridal supper for Tabitha and her mail-order groom.

Tabitha had devised a menu that Anke felt was less than befitting of an *Amisch* wedding supper. And there would not even be an eck or place of honor for the couple to sit. Moreover, there were no guests invited. Tabitha had reassured Anke that there could be a small celebration sometime after her *fater* returned from the deep woods and had accepted the groom of her choosing.

Anke moved about the spacious kitchen, praying that things might *geh* well between Tabitha and her chosen groom. It seemed to Anke that Tabitha was hardly *auld* enough to marry. She clearly recalled Tabitha as a young child, eager to make apple sauce or learn to scrape potatoes. Anke had done her best to be a substitute *mamm* to the little *maedel*, but she knew in her heart that Tabitha could be as headstrong as her *fater*.

Chapter Two

Matthew glanced at Abner, who regarded him with the same tense expression he'd worn for the duration of the past three days. "Do you always look like that?" Matthew asked, returning the knife he'd used to shave to the *aulder* man.

"Like what?"

"Ach, I don't know. . . . Mad, sad, ambivalent . . ."

Abner shook his hulking frame and grimaced. "Keep a civil tongue in your head, *buwe*. I've told ya who and what I am. Now move. We need to get to the big clearing and then on to Bishop Kore's before—"

The *aulder* man broke off in midsentence, and Matthew glanced at him with open curiosity. "Before what?"

"Never mind. Ya came here to marry, and, if she'll have you, marry ya shall."

Matthew shook his wet head. "Yes, I shall." He extended an arm. "Lead on, grim specter."

Abner glared at him but turned, and Matthew followed, wondering what he'd truly gotten himself into. . . .

* * *

The rushing creek muffled the sounds of the forest and soothed Tabitha's unusually tense mood. It was not that she was anxious about meeting Matthew King; *nee*, her *fater* had paraded at least a dozen men before her eyes, hoping that she would marry someone of his choosing. *Nee*, it was the stranger in the creek who'd unsettled her; there was something about him that tugged at her.

But she thrust away such thoughts and began to pace the pine-needled floor of the clearing in her black shoes, giving a quick tug to the pristine apron at the front of her pale yellow dress. She'd wanted to look her best, planned on it; now she wondered if Matthew King would stand in awe of her beauty—the way many men did. For Tabitha, it wasn't vanity; it was practicality. She wanted to know if the stiffness of his written response would melt beneath her gaze. Would he be smitten? She felt it would give her a measure of control in the relationship, and control was always *gut*.

She flicked absently at a *kapp* string as she moved. She knew that for the Mountain *Amisch*, marriage was a lasting thing and, in truth, she had no desire to be bound to some lout. She swallowed hard when she reflected on her own boldness in creating the ad and then drafting a carefully worded acceptance. *But if he seems ugly in his heart, or a beast of a fellow, I shall simply have Abner drive him off. I've committed to nothing. . . .* She ignored the niggle of doubt she felt, then stopped her pacing as Abner stepped from the laurel bushes with a tall man behind him.

Whatever she'd expected, it was not the handsome man she'd met that morning at the creek. She frowned as she took in his drying hair, now a rich, russet color rather than the dark, soapy strands she remembered. His eyes were

an intense green and she felt consumed by his gaze. She
was disconcerted and not at all used to the feeling. Then
she remembered her resolve to marry on her own terms,
and when he held out a large hand, she took it with a
direct look. His fingers were warm and enclosed hers for
a brisk, businesslike moment, and then he drew away.

She swallowed and spoke clearly. "Herr King. I'm
Tabitha Stolfus." *Your wife-to-be . . . Wife. Wife. Wife . . .*
She didn't say it, but she felt as if the word hung in the
air between them.

"It's a pleasure to meet you . . . properly, I should say."
He smiled down at her. "*Sei se gut*, call me Matthew."

His voice was deep and resonant. Strangely, she couldn't
help but compare him to other men—nee, *buwes*—in
Blackberry Falls. He stood with a commanding presence
and was a *gut* head taller than herself.

"At least you are bathed and dressed *properly* for the
ceremony." It was a firm declaration, with only the
faintest hint of sarcasm, as her gaze took in his white
shirt, dark suspenders, and black pants. His damp shirt
clung to his chest and shoulders, and she felt herself
frown.

But to her surprise, despite her attitude, she sensed a
relaxation in him, almost as if his damp shoulders shook
with laughter, and she couldn't resist speaking.

"You find something funny, Herr . . . Matthew?"

"*Nee* . . . I'm glad my attire suits you."

Tabitha immediately felt herself flush at his soft teasing but then straightened her spine. "*Jah*, it does. And
now we must hurry. Bishop Kore will be waiting."

But once more she felt confused by him when he considered her with a quizzical smile. She had to resist the

strange urge to reach up a hand to see if her *kapp* was on straight.

"Your prayer covering is on perfectly, Tabitha. But, I wonder—are we to marry with such haste? Surely you want to see if I fit your needs."

Tabitha stared at him, rallying the driving force inside her—to marry on her own terms. "You seem adequate," she said in deliberate, honeyed tones.

"*Danki*." He smiled. "But perhaps we could have a few minutes alone to discuss . . . adequacy?" She watched his gaze flick to the silent Abner, and she gave a reluctant nod of assent.

The *aulder* man came forward and stabbed a finger at Matthew's chest. "If ya so much as lay one finger—"

"I understand."

Tabitha watched her soon-to-be husband step away from the accusatory finger and nod his head respectfully. Then Abner grunted and walked away into the forest, and Tabitha readied herself to meet alone with her mail-order groom for the second time that morning.

If Tabitha Stolfus had meant to awe Matthew with her beauty once more, she could not have done a better job. Up close, her *Amisch* dress was the rich color of creamed butter and concealed though still hinted at her fine form and pert bosom. Her slender neck seemed incapable of supporting the mass of honey-blond hair that was mostly hidden beneath her *kapp*. But he hadn't missed the errant tendrils that had escaped to frame her oval face. Wide, sapphire-blue eyes looked up at him with a coolness he supposed was meant to be intimidating to a man, but their depths only made him wonder how blue they'd become when she'd been warmed by kissing.

He blinked, then shook himself mentally. He was here because of her *fater*'s woodworking—*nee* other reason. *As I told my* bruder . . . *she's incidental and only that.* Still, it was difficult to dismiss her beauty, and he watched her perfectly formed lips closely as she prepared to speak.

"According to tradition, a mail-order groom . . . is prepared to marry upon arrival and the meeting of his bride." She lowered her voice. "Now, tell me, do you find me adequate, Herr King?"

Her question sent a rush of warmth down his spine, but he answered with a coolness he didn't feel. "Surely, but there is always more to beauty than the exterior, Tabitha. Like a pine veneer that hides a wealth of burled elm, true beauty lies within."

"That's not what most men think," she muttered.

"What was that?"

"Nothing." She shook her head. "You speak knowledgeably of woodwork."

It was more a question than an observation, but he'd rehearsed this scenario in his mind. He shrugged. "I learned basic furniture making from my *fater*."

"Did you enjoy it?"

Did I enjoy it? Now that's a question I wasn't expecting. . . . On the one hand, he loved every minute he'd worked with wood, but his *fater* had stripped away most of the joy in the process. His *daed* had also limited the family business to making the most basic of furniture, with little-to-no-room for true creative craftsmanship. He supposed his *daed* was bitter after his *mamm*'s death; he'd certainly been brutal.

Matthew needed to answer her but was saved from having to reply when a tall, gangly man joined them in the clearing. The fellow fixed his beady eyes on Tabitha, and Matthew felt an unfamiliar flare of irritation as he stepped in front of his soon-to-be *frau*.

"Go on with you," he ordered harshly, even as he heard a sigh of frustration from behind him. Clearly, Tabitha had tangled with this beak-nosed *Amischer* in the past.

"Do you think I'd leave this delicate flower alone with some stranger?" The man's squeak of a voice grated on Matthew's nerves. "I happen to have once held the privilege of being betrothed to Tabitha, and I am not so far removed as to think that she is beyond my protection."

Matthew blinked as Tabitha stepped in front of him. "Elam, we were never betrothed; only my *fater* thought so. Now, why don't you just go on your way?"

"And leave you defenseless?"

Matthew thought he could see actual steam coming off Tabitha's head and hid a sudden smile. Clearly, the fellow didn't know what Matthew intuitively understood about the strength of the woman he'd met only that morning. *She's about to blow her stack. . . .*

"I am not defenseless. Now, please. . . . I've got private business with this man."

With his prominent Adam's apple, Elam appeared to gobble, but then Abner came back into the fray. And with one gloomy glare from Tabitha's guardian, Elam wavered away into the woods, leaving Matthew a clear field to tease Tabitha as she turned back to face him.

"A disgruntled man—a broken betrothal?" He reached

out a hand to lightly skim a finger down her rosy cheek. "What am I to think?"

She slapped away his hand, and he laughed.

"You wouldn't be laughing if you knew what a tittering gossip Elam Smucker is!"

"What's there to gossip about?" Matthew asked lightly. "We're only getting married."

He smothered another laugh when she glared up at him and would have said more if Abner hadn't grunted his disapproval.

"Enough of this playin'. Bishop Kore is waiting and we don't have much time."

The *aulder* man's words sobered Matthew's mood as he wondered again about the hurry.

Tabitha turned around on the steps where she stood outside Bishop Kore's cabin; she couldn't deny that Matthew King was more than handsome. He moved with a lithe, pantherlike grace when he walked, and his hair had dried to an even brighter russet color that she couldn't help but find pleasing. As he drew closer, she could see his green eyes and covertly took in his broad shoulders, narrow waist, and long legs.

Something of her thoughts must have shown on her face, though, because he mounted the carved wooden steps behind Abner and stopped to gaze down at her.

"Would you like to examine my teeth?" he asked politely.

"What?"

"My teeth?" He gave her a wolfish grin, baring strong,

white teeth. "Wasn't that in the ad? I thought because you were evaluating the rest of me . . ."

She frowned darkly, a sharp retort coming to her lips, but then, she didn't want to give him the satisfaction of knowing that he'd riled her, so she held her tongue.

The opening of the bishop's door reminded her that her wedding was nigh, and she arranged her features into the semblance of a smile. Bishop Kore was an odd, forgetful man until it was time for him to speak during church service; then his voice thundered with certainty. But now he stood with the door open, a congenial if somewhat confused expression on his *auld* face.

"Ach, Tabitha and the *gut* Abner. But who else do we have here?"

Tabitha wanted to grit her teeth at the bishop's forgetfulness, but she smiled sweetly instead. "This is Matthew King. We're here to be married. Do you recall that I spoke with you in private some days past?"

"Marriage? *Jah*, a sober state to enter into. Nothing like fruit salad . . . Well, *kumme* in. *Kumme* right in."

Tabitha ignored the strange mention of fruit salad—the bishop's peculiarities were of little concern to her at the moment. She swallowed and followed the *auld* man into his modest cabin, very conscious of Matthew King at her back.

"May we hurry, Herr Bishop?" she asked, frustrated when the man was distracted by Matthew's apparent interest in the carving of one of the key support beams in the cabin.

She watched as he touched the oak beam with strong

hands, then smiled at the bishop. "A cabin such as this is built like a rock, sir. No storm could shake it, I think."

Bishop Kore gave a wheezing laugh. "Built *on* a rock, my *buwe*. As sure as sunfish. You're interested in woodworking? Well, *Derr Herr* must surely have made your match with Tabitha. Her *fater* is—"

"Not here!" Tabitha snapped, then amended her tone. "Of course not, Herr Bishop. He's deep in the high timber. Don't you recall? Not here. Not for another day, I hope. . . . I mean . . . surely he'll be returning soon. If we could just proceed . . . right now!"

Chapter Three

Silence snapped in the room as three pairs of male eyes swung in Tabitha's direction at her abrupt order, which was so unlike an *Amisch* woman's usual behavior. She met them with a demure look, trying to control the blush she knew stained her cheeks. She forged on with determination. "Don't you agree that we should hurry, Herr . . . uh . . . Matthew?"

The man had the temerity to raise a dark brow at her as a faint smile played about his mouth. Indeed, he crossed the floor and put an arm around her waist, pulling her subtly into the damp warmth of his side. She longed to struggle, but then remembered that time was passing and turned innocent blue eyes up to meet his gaze.

"*Jah, mei* sweet," he agreed in warm tones. "Why, I can hardly count the hours until tonight when we shall both drink . . . from the goblet of love."

"Ahem!" Abner choked, while Tabitha frowned and shook her head at him. Then she looked at the astonished bishop; the man simply had to hurry. . . . There was always the chance that her *fater* might return early from his expedition. She would breathe a lot easier when the wedding was over.

Matthew felt the tension in her body as he held her to his side. He wished she'd relax. Yet it was a pleasurable thing, the rather intimate touch of a woman, something he hadn't experienced in a long while.

"Are you ordering me about, *mei maedel*?" Bishop Kore had adopted the subdued roar he must use during church services, and Matthew hugged her closer. He doubted that she was usually so abrupt and he admired her impulsive words—words that had effectively brought the bishop back to the moment for whatever reason she might have.

"I do not recall you ever being of such a disposition when we spoke earlier, Tabitha!" the *auld* man thundered.

"I assume full responsibility for the hurry, *gut* Bishop," Matthew put in smoothly. "I am twenty-seven, alone in the area, and, I admit, besotted by such *Gott*-given beauty as Tabitha's. Just look at her skin—like fresh cream, is it not? And her eyes, as blue as jewels in the sunshine . . . Why her shape alone is—"

Bishop Kore cleared his throat and then began the ceremony in haste, almost as though the *auld* man wanted to put behind them any sin the two might have already committed.

Matthew listened with only half an ear to the High German the bishop spoke as he began the marriage ceremony. And somehow, what usually took three hours and involved hundreds of guests and at least six baked hams was over in a matter of minutes. He'd given his assent, as had Tabitha, and he was now officially a mail-order groom and husband. He glanced down at Tabitha's face, expecting to see some evidence of a smile, but instead, he encountered a look of almost grim satisfaction. He wondered at her expression and then decided he wasn't much better on the getting-what-you-want scale.

Here I've married the maedel *out of a desire to learn from her* fater, *who is clearly the person she wants independence from, yet somehow I've got to pretend that she, herself, is the main reason for my agreeing to the arrangement.*

"It's done, then," Abner said, breaking into Matthew's thoughts.

"*Jah*," Bishop Kore agreed, clearly relieved. "As done as a fish on an evening fry."

"We're two done fish," Tabitha quipped as she wriggled away from Matthew's arm. "Now, we must be going, I'm afraid. *Danki*, Bishop Kore. Abner, can you please give the bishop that envelope?"

Matthew watched Abner hand the *auld* man a white envelope, which obviously contained a gift of money of some sort. It seemed a strange thing to do—normally, an *Amisch* bishop performed his duties without payment. Perhaps Tabitha was merely being generous.

Bishop Kore nodded his thanks, then gestured toward another finely crafted door in his living room. "*Kumme.* I would be the first to congratulate the young couple with a gift."

"Perhaps something to soothe your impatience?" Matthew whispered to Tabitha.

"I'm not impatient, you lout!" she hissed, then immediately looked appalled at what she'd said.

He had to struggle not to laugh. If nothing else, his new *frau* had a fiery temper, and he wondered idly if she displayed such spirit in front of her *fater*.

Tabitha felt her hands shake a bit and she clasped them before her as she followed Bishop Kore into his small study. For whatever reason, Matthew King—der *mann*— her husband, rattled her in a way that she did not appreciate or understand. And she found herself wondering at the way he took her ill humor in stride—he didn't appear offended, but rather seemed to be enjoying himself when she felt ready to box his ears.

She drew her attention back to the moment as they approached Bishop Kore's cluttered desk. Papers were stuck willy-nilly in drawers, while others were stacked here and there in haphazard piles; yet the bishop seemed to know exactly what he was looking for under the mess. He slid out a rock, about the breadth of his hand, and held it out to her.

"Here it is. I found it at the top of the falls one day. I nearly fell over trying to reach it, but *Derr Herr* righted my footing."

Tabitha took the rock, thinking it to be simply another odd notion of the bishop, but then she looked closer at its smooth surface.

"Now, what do you see?" Bishop Kore asked softly.

She felt Matthew lean over her shoulder as she tried to concentrate. "I—I see shells. Seashells. Or the imprints of shells at least, somehow embedded into the rock."

"Fossils," Matthew said, reaching down to gently stroke one of the impressions with a lean finger. "Proof of the biblical flood—to find seashell fossils at the top of so high a mountain."

"Aha!" The bishop slapped his thigh, startling Tabitha with the abrupt sound; she took a step backward and bumped unceremoniously into her new husband's strong body. It was like hitting an oak tree at full tilt, and she tried to ignore the sensation.

"So what do—fossils—have to do with our marriage?" she asked somewhat irritably.

"They don't belong here, *kind*, yet they do." Bishop Kore smiled at her, but she couldn't make any sense of the *auld* man's words.

"Is it a riddle?" Matthew asked with obvious interest.

"*Jah*, but not one to be solved with ease. *Gott* must reveal the answer to each of you, much like a dumped gelatin mold—I prefer green myself."

Tabitha handed the rock to Matthew and nodded her thanks to the bishop. She had one more phase of her mail-order-groom plan to complete and she could ill afford to waste any more time. "We will take our leave now," she said in a firm voice, expecting, for some reason, that Matthew might contradict her. But her new husband merely shook the bishop's hand, then gently took her arm as they left, with Abner leading the way.

Abner was more than grateful for the cup of coffee Anke poured for him after he'd seen Tabitha and her new husband back to the Stolfus cabin.

"She took him to her room," Anke confided in nervous tones.

Abner waved off her concern with a slightly weary

hand. "Just as I expected. The *maedel* knows what she wants and will not rest until she has it."

"I offered her the wedding supper, but she said it would have to be kept warm for a bit."

Abner frowned, not liking to see Anke upset, but he also knew that Tabitha would take no risk of a possible annulment either. He knew exactly why she'd led Matthew King to her room.

"Well," he said after an awkward moment. "Why not let me sample some of yer supper? I'm sure it's *gut*, and I be more than hungry." He shifted on the kitchen bench, admitting to one hunger but denying another. Anke's movements from stove to table were brisk and confident, though her pretty face still looked worried, and he longed to ease her mind.

Chapter Four

As she and Matthew stood in the middle of her bedroom, Tabitha had to resist the urge to bite her bottom lip—an *auld* habit that she'd tried to break but that still presented itself when she was highly nervous. *I have no reason to be nervous*, she thought, as cool practicality took over her mind once more. *I understand what happens in the marriage bed, and once our union is consummated, my choice of a husband will be secure.*

She gave a swift look at Matthew and swallowed before lifting her chin. "Would you turn around, *sei se gut*?"

He gave her a quizzical glance. "Why?"

She felt herself flush. "So that I may . . . remove my dress. Or better yet, I shall *geh* behind the dressing screen." Relieved, she started across the hardwood floor, but her new husband stepped in her path.

She looked up into his green eyes and struggled to match their steady gaze. "You would consummate the marriage before we've even talked together?" he asked softly.

Tabitha stiffened her resolve. *I would consummate this marriage before my* fater *returns, but I cannot tell you that. . . .* "I would. Talking is something we will have a lifetime to do."

"We will. That's true." He reached a lean finger to the curve of her cheek and she felt herself flush, startled that such a simple touch could make her feel as if she was being drenched with warm honey.

But despite this secret pleasure, she stepped away from him and quickly sidled past to reach the relative safety of the dressing screen. Once there, she began to automatically take the pins from her dress and apron, ignoring the sudden, frantic beating of her heart.

Matthew wandered idly about the large room, trying to ignore the faint rustling of clothing that came to him from behind the dressing screen. He stopped at the huge sleigh bed and reached down to trail the back of his hand across the flimsy batiste shift that lay waiting on the thick, rose-patterned quilt. Things were going way too fast, but he'd signed on for this—quite literally at that.

"Would you mind passing me my shift?" Tabitha asked, and he could almost hear the steel in her tone.

He turned and handed the thin shift over the top of the screen, trying to ignore the sudden rush of images that invaded his mind. *She will be lovely, beyond compare perhaps, but I don't love her . . . not yet anyway . . . not ever maybe. I will have the wood as my mistress, and that will be enough. . . .* He ignored the dart of doubt that passed through his mind, then turned and caught his breath as Tabitha emerged from behind the screen.

The late-afternoon sunshine illuminated the length and

color of her shining hair, while her beautiful eyes were wide with determination. The shift did more to reveal than conceal the perfection of her high breasts, slim waist, and gently curved belly and hips. In truth, he'd never seen anyone so beautiful, but he took an automatic step backward, as if to avoid the spell of her loveliness.

If she noticed his movement, she ignored it completely and strode with her head lifted and her hair brushing the curved outline of her bottom, directly to her bed. She stepped with spritelike grace on a footstool to reach the fluffy mattress, and Matthew found himself helplessly following the flow of her body even as she lay down on her back with visible tension. He saw that she steeled herself to be still.

"I'm ready," she gritted out. "You may proceed and get this over with."

He stared down at her; her forced words started a pounding behind his eyes. He hadn't lived a chaste life, but never had a woman so blatantly offered herself to him. He stepped to the edge of the bed and reached to splay his hand gently across her slender belly. Then he looked deep into the twin pools of her sapphire-blue eyes. "Get this over with?" he asked hoarsely. "Are you so sure, then, that you are a mere sacrifice to be had once and done?"

He watched her frown. Clearly, she hadn't thought about all of the other *nachts* when he might now choose to exercise his bedding rights. . . . He lifted his hand and almost idly trailed a finger from her pulsing throat to the top curve of her breast. It would be so easy to accept what she readily offered, but something held him back. He wasn't ready yet to be a mail-order groom in both truth and deed. . . .

Tabitha resisted the urge to squeeze shut her eyes and watched him touch her, his green gaze intent. She almost jumped when he sat down on the bed next to her. The strong length of his leg pressed against her hip, and she felt unaccountably hot at this touch. She cleared her throat and her voice come out strangely high and breathy.

"*Kumme*," she said with deliberate, womanly softness. "Let us finalize our vows."

She watched him slowly shake his head and knew a moment of deep frustration. If he would not consummate the marriage, she had not completely succeeded in marrying the man of her choosing. But she recognized determination when she saw it, and Matthew King was not so ruled by desire that he forgot his principles, evidently.

She blew out a sharp breath, then slapped an irritated hand on the soft pile of quilts beneath her. "Am I not attractive enough?" she asked, her voice verging on sarcasm. But then she wondered if perhaps he truly did not find her pleasing, and she felt shaken.

"Attractive?" He gave a rueful laugh and lifted one of her golden curls to his mouth, then lowered her hair quickly. "In truth, I have never seen anyone so lovely."

Mollified, she nonetheless glared at him. "Then why do you wait?"

"I wait—because I will not make love to you without knowing you first."

"That's ridiculous," she burst out, and he smiled.

"Don't fear, *mei frau*. To the rest of the world we will

act as if we are husband and wife. I don't want to bring you shame, but I will sleep on the floor and you in the bed, and we will . . . talk."

"Talk?" she snapped. "A mail-order groom is supposed to—"

"Ach, *jah*, tell me what a mail-order groom is supposed to do?" he asked wryly. "To my knowledge, I may be the first of my kind and can therefore make up my own rules."

Tabitha huffed at his reply. *I make the rules*, she thought, but then spoke sweetly. "Very well, but no one outside this room may know. And no one must know about the ad or that you're a mail-order groom."

"I give you my word." He rose from the bed and offered her a hand up.

She was conscious of his eyes upon her and immediately began to scheme how she might satisfy his *narrisch* idea of getting to know each other. . . .

Chapter Five

As Matthew followed Tabitha down the curved stair-case, his mind and focus were torn in two different directions—a fascination with the patina of the wood of the bannister beneath his hand and the painful realiza-tion that he had just passed up the opportunity of bed-ding his wife. In the end, though, it was the look on *auld* Abner's face, from where he stood at the bottom of the staircase, that snapped him out of his deliberations.

If possible, Aber appeared more dour than usual, and Matthew watched as the *aulder* man took Tabitha's hand and paused to search her face. *Probably looking for some sign of abuse on my part*, Matthew thought.

He reached the bottom of the stairs and effectively in-serted himself between Tabitha and her guardian, sliding an arm around her tiny waist. "Everything is right as rain, is it not, my sweet?"

He watched as Tabitha turned to look up at him with a warm smile on her pink mouth. "*Jah*, most certainly."

He couldn't help giving her a wry glance and then im-mediately banished it by bending to brush her lips with a brief kiss. She wanted to resist; he felt this instinctively in the sudden tension of her back, but then he lifted his head and gave Abner a sunny smile.

The other man let out a breath of palpable frustration, but whatever he had been going to say was lost in the moment as the front door was thrust open from the outside. A booming voice echoed from the vaulted wooden ceiling of the hall and a large man with a walking stick limped inside. A small bulldog gamboled about his legs and then ran toward Abner, who gruffly put out a hand to the barking creature.

Matthew watched in silence as Tabitha broke from his hold and went to the other *Amisch* man.

"Ach, Da . . . you're home!"

Tabitha knew a sudden pounding in her heart as she lightly embraced her *fater*. This was the moment she had been waiting for, and it was with not a little trepidation that she hastened her *fater* inside and scooped up Ralph, the bulldog puppy, to snuggle him against her chest.

"Abner," her *fater* said, shaking her guardian's outstretched hand. "We found a fine stand of red oak."

"That's *gut*, John."

"And who is this?" Her *fater* gestured to Matthew.

Tabitha held her breath, unsure of how this all-important meeting would *geh*. She hurried to Matthew's side. Her new *mann* was a *gut* head taller than her *daed*, but her *fater* was bulkier.

"*Fater, sei se gut*, I'd like to introduce Matthew King." She put down the dog and gestured to the tall man beside her.

"Matt, nice to know you, and given the fact that my

dochder has allowed you within ten feet of her, I'd say you're someone special."

"*Jah*, Da." Tabitha lifted her chin. "Matthew is my husband. We married today."

She watched her *fater*'s blue eyes widen in shock, then fill unexpectedly with tears. "Your . . . husband? Tabby, is it true?" He caught her hands and pulled her into a tight embrace. "Ach, what am I doing? Matt—at long last. A *sohn*!" He widened his arms to embrace Matthew as well.

Tabitha told herself she was pleased with how well her *fater* had received the news, but something rankled still the same. *A* sohn *at last. . . . A* sohn *. . . Is this why my da has been so anxious to marry me off? To have a* sohn, *a* sohn *to inherit the mill and run it as he sees fit . . . with no thought to my own knowledge of timber or business. . . .* It was ridiculous, but somehow, at that moment, she felt jealous of her own husband.

Matthew had seen the injured look Tabitha had quickly masked, and he knew that, in some way, her *fater*, in his jubilation, had wounded her. Matthew told himself that he could not begin to plumb the depths of a woman's mind, and Tabitha Stolfus, *nee*, King was more of a woman than most. Still, it bothered him, and he realized he'd been too absorbed in his own thoughts to notice that the small group that had seated themselves around the wedding supper table had grown rather silent.

He looked up, feeling himself flush, and addressed his new *fater*-in-law. "I'm sorry, sir. What was that?"

Herr Stolfus waved a fork at him. "I asked you how you and my *dochder* first met."

Matthew knew he could ill afford to bungle his response, and the sudden wariness in his wife's sapphire-blue eyes added to the pressure.

"We've grown our relationship through letters, sir."

"Letters? *Jah*. . . ." Herr Stolfus took a massive bite of whipped potatoes. "But the first time you laid eyes on each other, *buwe*? When was that?"

Abner cleared his throat, and Matthew shot him a quick glance. Surely Tabitha's guardian would not betray the truth about the ad.

"It wuz me, John, that first introduced them. In the woods it wuz," Abner said finally.

Matthew held his breath, and then John Stolfus nodded. "A happy meeting, I take it?"

"*Jah*," Abner muttered.

Apparently, it was enough of an answer to content his new *fater*-in-law, and Matthew drew a relieved sigh; he saw that his young wife, sitting opposite him at the table, clearly felt the same relief. Then Anke bustled in with another platter of roast beef, and the talk drifted to the red oak that had been found.

"Do you know lumber, *buwe*?" Herr Stolfus asked.

Matthew shrugged casually. "A bit about furniture making and the like." *It was true, technically. I don't know as much about woodworking as I want . . . After all, that's why I'm here.* Still, the half-truth tasted bitter now for some reason, but he shook off the thought.

"Well, I say, *sohn*, that the best way to learn is on the job! Right, Abner?"

"Sure, John."

"So, Matt, you'll accompany the *buwes* on the logging trip to get the red oak. I'll have them head out in the next day or two. Gives you only a bit of time for a honeymoon, eh, Tabby? That's what the *Englischers* call it, don't they?"

Matthew watched as Tabitha turned a serene face to her *fater*. "They do indeed. But while *mei mann* is gone, would you mind if Abner took me up to Aenti Fern's cabin? I might stay with her for a bit, and Abner can have a break." She glanced across the table. "But I suppose it's you, Matthew, who must now permit me to go. . . ."

"Me?" he asked, confused.

"*Jah*, you are my husband. And in the ways of our community, a wife must gain permission from her *mann* to do such a thing as be away from home and hearth for such a time."

Home and hearth, my foot. The little minx is plotting, but I suppose it's her affair. . . . "*Jah*, then by all means *geh*. Is Aenti Fern your sister, sir?" He turned to his host.

"Hmm? *Nee, nee, buwe*. Aenti Fern is the healer in these parts. A strange creature, but Tabby has always taken to her."

"I see. Well then, *mei frau*, enjoy yourself, *sei se gut*."

"Ach, *danki*, Matthew. I know I shall."

She smiled at him, and he blinked. *She is definitely up to something. . . .*

Chapter Six

"So, yer *fater* bids me to attend ya, on yer wedding *nacht*, mind. . . . and what else am I ta do but prepare ya for a *nacht* with a man ya know nuthin' about?" Anke drew the brush through Tabitha's long hair and clucked nervously.

"Don't fret so, Anke. Everything's going as planned." *Well, not everything. Not if Matthew sleeps on the floor. . . .* For all her *fater*'s enthusiasm over the marriage, she still wanted the arrangement between her and her new *mann* to be her choice—sealed and done. *And I have a plan for that . . .*

Anke soon finished her hair and, with a parting sigh, left Tabitha in peace. But peace was not what she sought as she slipped out of her robe and turned down all but one lantern. She moved in the muted light, biting her lip and wondering whether she might present a more alluring pose standing rather than lying in bed. But the choice was made for her when she heard footsteps in the hall. She jumped into bed and curled up like a kitten beneath the quilt, her eyes closed as she feigned sleep.

She tried to remain relaxed as she heard the door open

and close and then booted steps cross the room. After a few moments, she wondered at the lack of sound and was a second from taking a peek. . . .

Her eyes flew open as the quilt was neatly pulled from atop her. She saw it flap, then drop to the floor.

"Ach!" She sat up with a jerk, a frown on her lips, when her husband pulled one of the goose-feather pillows from behind her back.

"I'm glad I didn't wake you." He laughed.

She glared up at him and hugged the edges of her shift around her, watching him as he lowered his suspenders and began to work the hook and eye closures on his shirt. Against her will, she followed the movements of his lean fingers in the mellow light.

"Only my shirt, all right?" he asked, easing the cloth from his shoulders.

"I'd rather it be more," she said, daring a bit of humor, and he smiled at her as he dropped to his knees on the stolen quilt.

She almost smiled back, but then something chased across her mind. "You asked me why I wrote the ad. . . . Why did you answer it? Is there someone back home you loved and lost? Is that why you don't want to consummate the marriage?" The possibility bothered her, but she had to ask. She didn't like the idea of being a second choice.

He sighed and shook his head. "*Nee*, my curious wife. I meant what I said this afternoon. I want us to know each other better."

"And the truth as to why you answered the ad?"

* * *

Matthew lay down on the quilt on his back and flung an arm over his eyes. *What am I to say?* He heard once more the echo of his glib words to his *bruder*. . . . *incidental. That's all she is* . . . but here he'd discovered a flesh-and-blood woman, with strength and purpose, who wanted him as her husband in truth. . . .

"I wanted a change. I saw your ad and your words . . . spoke to me." He closed his eyes hard as he uttered the lie, grateful to put it behind him. *She need never know*, he reasoned. *But Gott knows . . . Gott knows. . . .* "Tell me something of your Blackberry Falls," he said hoarsely, hoping to change the subject.

He heard her soft sigh in the stillness of the room. "Blackberry Falls is—a strange place, I suppose."

"In what way?"

He heard her sheets rustle. "Well, you've met Bishop Kore. . . ."

He laughed softly. "That's true. What's his story? Is he married?"

"He was, long ago. My *fater* remembers his *frau*. She died when I was but a babe."

"And your own *mamm*, Tabitha?"

"She passed after nursing Bishop Kore's wife. There were fifteen people in all who died from influenza that year. My *fater* will only speak of it if I ask him. And I don't ask him often. . . ."

Matthew cleared his throat. "Your *daed* seems to be happy that we've wed, but I noticed your face when he exclaimed over now having a *sohn*. How did you feel about—"

"I'm tired, Matthew. I'll *geh* to sleep now."

He nodded in the muted light, even though she couldn't see him, and the minutes passed as he struggled to fall asleep himself. It was not until she turned down the lantern by her bedside that he could find refuge in the darkness and finally close his eyes. . . .

Although his cabin was not far from the Stolfus *haus*, Abner drowsed by the fire after John went to bed. He was relaxed for the moment, after the stress of the evening. Still, he nearly jumped from the chair when Anke came soft-footed into the room.

"Well, I suppose that went as well as it might," Anke whispered as she straightened the kerosene lamp on the cherry end table.

"*Jah*," he whispered back, tense as always in her presence. He rubbed absently at the back of his neck, seeking something to say. She caught him completely off guard when she regarded him with a concerned expression.

"Does your neck pain you, Abner?"

"My . . . neck . . . ?" He lowered his hand slowly as rapid thoughts fired through his brain. *What if I lie and say* jah—*what might she do?* "I . . . don't—"

"Here now. You've had yer hands full the last few days. Lemme give ya a bit of a neck rub. . . . That's if you'd like . . ."

She drifted off, and he realized he would probably hurt her if he refused, not that he had any desire to refuse. *To have her touch me would be . . .*

She bustled behind the rocker and he felt her carefully roll down the back of his collar. He shivered, unsure of what to do with his hands; he settled for clenching the arms of the chair. Then she touched him, and he felt his belly tighten and his face flush. He couldn't remember the last time someone had touched him with kindness or warmth, and he was surprised to feel his eyes well with tears at the sensation.

Her fingers brushed the nape of his neck. "Yer hair's a bit long. . . . I can cut it fer ya tomorrow if ya *kumme* round."

"*Jah*," he choked, unable to get anything else out.

Anke swallowed hard as she found the tight knots of tension in Abner's strong neck. She realized that she'd been uncommonly bold to ask to help him, but to tell the truth, she wished that someone would rub her own neck. She knew that if she had a headache, Abner must surely feel worse after the stress of the day.

Still, it felt odd to be so close to him, but the idea of closeness always created anxiety within her. As usual, she found it was easier to avoid closeness than to fight the rising panic.

"There," she muttered. "I hope that helped."

"*Jah*," he said, low. "I—I could do the same for you, Anke. I know today was hard."

"*Nee*," she said abruptly. "I be fine." *Fine . . . fine . . . but I'm not, and I surely never will be.*

Chapter Seven

Tabitha turned on the brittle-edged stone steps that led to Aenti Fern's cabin. The healer's *haus* was rather remote, which suited Tabitha's plans perfectly. "You can *geh* on back, Abner. I will be fine from here."

"I'll *kumme* for ya day after tomorrow."

Tabitha nodded, then turned away to hurry up the steps. She had no time to lose. Matthew had left at least an hour earlier with a team of men set on harvesting the red oak hardwood. She had waved him away with a smile, and she refused to contemplate the warm kiss he'd given her before he mounted Gray, one of her favorite geldings.

Now she knocked briefly on the carved wooden door of the awkward little stone cottage and was about to knock again when Aenti Fern called, "*Kumme* in."

Tabitha entered the fragrant place, in which she always felt she must duck her head to avoid the great array of herbs and flowers that hung drying from the rafters. She did so now, then straightened to *geh* and embrace the bent-backed *auld* woman who was working away, stirring a concoction on the small woodstove.

"Ach, Aenti Fern, there's so much I need to tell you, but I—"

"*Jah, kind*, very much, I think, but your thoughts are racing with something more pressing, are they not?"

"*Jah*." Fern smiled. "I need to borrow Huntress and I need you to turn me into a *buwe*. . . ."

Abner wound his way through the forest from Aenti Fern's cottage, glad to be alone with his thoughts for the moment. He told himself that he could cut his own hair, the way he usually did, by hacking it off with a knife. But a real haircut, under Anke's kind hands, would be such a treat. And after all, she'd offered. . . .

Half an hour later, he found himself on John's wide back porch, while Ralph the bulldog barked to herald his presence. Anke opened the back door and Abner felt himself give her a sheepish grin.

"You said yesterday ta *kumme* round if I—"

"Needed a haircut. *Jah*, Abner, have a seat out here and I'll *geh* get my things." When Anke turned back inside, Abner sat on one of the ladder-back chairs on the porch and took Ralph up on his lap. The puppy rolled over to have his pink belly rubbed and snorted noisily. Abner put down the dog when Anke returned.

"Ach, *geh* on with ya, Ralphie," Anke scolded, though Abner could tell that she loved the little creature.

She flapped an *auld*, clean sheet smartly and settled it around the front of his neck, tying it at the back. Then he realized that she was feeling the texture of his hair, as if considering more than his usual haphazard style.

* * *

Anke's fingers slowed of their own accord. Once more, she found herself close to the man she admired, and she was determined not to run this time. *At least give him a fine haircut. . . .* She found that by concentrating on the soft thickness of his hair, she was able to focus on creating a suitable style while her anxiety was kept at a low simmer.

She took her time, despite the tense stillness he displayed and the tightness of his fine jaw. He'd never married, so he kept that jaw clean shaven, and she wondered why no woman had snapped him up as a *mann*.

She moved around to his front, while Ralph played beneath the sheet and Anke continued to cut and trim, whisking hair onto the sheet and porch. When she was finally satisfied, she lifted a small hand mirror up for him to see.

"Looks . . . fine. Really fine," he mumbled.

She clasped the mirror and put her hands on her hips, cocking her head to study him at length. "Ya do look *gut*, Abner . . . even if I say so meself."

Then she swept the sheet from his neck and shook out the hair onto the grass for the birds to use to make their nests.

The dew fell from the overhanging branches of the forest and the horses kicked up stones as they picked their way over the floor of the woods. The sun had yet to burn off the low-lying fog, and Matthew felt excitement in his chest as the group of men left Blackberry Falls far behind and slowly worked their way deeper into the mountains.

Matthew rode alongside a man toward the middle of the group of seven. Herr Stolfus had stayed behind to do paperwork. Matthew was grateful when the man riding next to him introduced himself as Big Jim. The nickname was apt, as the fellow had a barrel-like body, and Matthew felt faintly sorry for his horse. But Big Jim was affable and seemed to have taken no offense at the way John Stolfus had presented his new *sohn*-in-law that morning at the mill. Matthew inwardly cringed when he recalled the introduction.

Herr Stolfus had rushed him through breakfast, as eager to show off his new *sohn* as a giddy child with a toy at Christmas time. John had hustled him along the path to the mill, giving Matthew no chance to study the building before he was swept inside.

"*Buwes*!" John had called. "Gather round! Rejoice with me. . . . My *dochder* has finally married and I have a new *sohn*! I want you all to treat him as such, as he will one day, as *Gott* wills, take my place as owner and boss of Stolfus Lumber and Woodworking!"

Matthew had the absurd notion that he should lift his hand and wave at the group of thirtysome men who stared back at him. Some seemed bemused, while others glared at him with outright disgust. He realized, in that instant, that what had started as his own selfish desire to learn woodworking with a master had become very complicated. There were people involved whose lives and livelihood might one day depend on him, and he felt like a fraud and an outsider standing before them. He was determined to do something about it.

Now, he tried to concentrate on what Big Jim was saying. "Back when Pennsylvania used to be called Penn's Woods, folks would say that ya could git from here ta West Virginia without puttin' a foot on the ground—the trees wuz so thick together. Where you *kumme* from, I bet you've heard the same, haven't ya, Matt?"

Matthew smiled, thinking of similar lore he'd heard growing up. "It's true, though I grew up in a little town on the banks of the Susquehanna River. We were surrounded by mountains in the river valley, but the woods were nothing as deep and lush as this."

Big Jim nodded, seeming pleased with his answer, and they rode on together.

"Ach, a *buwe*, you say, Tabby girl?" Aenti Fern's wrinkled face wrinkled even more, until she looked like one of the dried apple dolls Tabitha used to make as a child.

"*Jah*, and I'm afraid it must be quick, Aenti Fern."

The *auld* woman laughed. "Such things take time. Now, show me your hands."

Tabitha frowned but knew there was no getting around one of Aenti Fern's requests. She held out her hands, palms up, and the *auld* woman gently touched the tips of her fingers.

"So, child, your secret continues I see. . . . Will you tell your new *mann*? I wonder."

"*Nee*, he wouldn't understand."

"Are you so sure?"

"*Jah*, now *sei se gut*, may we hurry?"

Aenti Fern sighed and turned away. "If we must. Take off your *kapp* and those shoes. . . ."

Chapter Eight

At the end of the day's trek, Asa Zook, the leader of the small group of Stolfus's men, called back that it was time to make camp for the *nacht*. Matthew had enjoyed the ride and was grateful for Big Jim's solid company, although the others had spoken only briefly to him.

With capable hands, Matthew took special care of Gray, the big gelding, then tied the hungry horse to some low-hanging branches so that he might graze to his heart's content. With his horse settled, Matthew made it a point to help wherever needed in setting up camp.

He bent to set a tent peg for Asa, but the taciturn man waved him off. "*Geh* on with ya, flatlander."

Matthew felt himself flush with irritation. To be called a "flatlander," or one who didn't *kumme* from the mountains, was a direct insult. Still, he was not about to give any sign of temper, which would only make things worse among the men.

He took a hatchet from the satchel Abner had handed him when they'd left and went deeper into the woods, where the summer moon played hide and seek with itself among the trees and mountain laurel. He intended to cut some firewood, but he paused for a moment as the moon-light shone on a mossy stone against a tall tree. He went and sat on the stone, leaning his back against the tree, and took a minute to pray.

Gott, *I don't know what I'm doing here. I thought it was so simple, but there are so many people here that I could hurt . . . not the least of whom is my* frau. *Bless her,* Fater. *Your thoughts are not my thoughts,* Gott. *Lead me through Herr, for Your Glory. . . ."*

Matthew bowed his head, ready to *geh* back to the camping site, when he heard a low voice begin to speak from somewhere close.

"It's bad enough that the brat had to choose a flat-lander—seems she thought she wuz too *gut* for the likes of us. But now, we're supposed to see him as the *sohn*— the heir and our boss, huh. . . . I bet he can't even whittle a toothpick. . . ."

Matthew listened intently, knowing they were dis-cussing him and Tabitha. He didn't want to eavesdrop, but making his presence known would only aggravate the situation.

Then another voice came—lower and filled with more anger. "I say there's many an accident in the woods— It might serve our future boss right if he met with a bit of trouble. . . ."

"Asa, what're ya talkin' about? We're *Amisch*, and ta intend ta harm another is—"

"Shut up, Micah. Ya always wuz a coward. . . . Now, hush. Here *kummes* Big Jim."

Matthew held his place, tense and motionless. He would have to be careful the next day when they cut the red oak; he had no desire to be someone's accident. . . .

He bowed his head to pray once more, but all that rang in his head and heart was the Bible promise he'd learned as a child . . . "No weapon formed against ye shall prosper . . ." He knew that *Gott* would help him somehow.

Tabitha and Aenti Fern's gray wolf dog, Huntress, had been following the group of men throughout the day in the cover of the deep woods. Huntress had a keen nose and was wise enough to hang back, lest they be discovered. And even if someone should see them, Tabitha knew that she looked just like another lumber *buwe* to the casual eye.

Aenti Fern had helped her bind her chest and had provided an outfit of *Amisch buwe*'s clothes, complete with the long, underwear shirt that most men wore in the woods because it kept them from being soaked with sweat and catching a chill. Some soot from the banked fire darkened her jaw like the beginnings of a beard and her hair was hidden under a tight cap. She moved on foot, knowing that a horse would likely give her away, but she was strong and fortified even more by the bitter elixir Aenti Ruth had made for her. In truth, it felt as if she could walk for days.

When the dark began to set in she found herself a cozy seat in a strong maple tree while Huntress lay down to silently guard the ground around the base of the tree. Tabitha was not afraid in the woods; Abner had seen to that. He'd often taken her on long rambles through the forest, pointing out which mushrooms were safe to eat and which ones could kill. He'd also shown her how to behave should she ever *kumme* across a mother bear and her cubs and how to treat a rattlesnake bite. But mostly, he'd shown her *Gott* as the Creator of the wondrous mountains and taught her that she could find kinship with Him there.

So, she unwrapped the corn muffins Aenti Fern had given her and munched away happily, dropping down a portion for Huntress to share. Tabitha could see the light of the men's fire and allowed herself to doze for a bit, not wanting to put her plan into action too soon.

Abner allowed himself the luxury of taking a stroll through the myriad paths of Blackberry Falls. He knew he could *geh* over to the Fisher General Store, or Cubby's, as it was called, and get into a checkers match, but he really felt himself to be at loose ends. Restless, he stuffed his hands into his pockets and turned the corner around a small pine, nearly running smack-dab into Bishop Kore.

Abner wanted to groan. The *gut* bishop was a fine speaker at church meetings, but on a daily basis, a fella never quite knew how to respond to the *auld* man.

"Ach, Abner, how are you on this evening of raining cows?"

Abner glanced briefly at the clear, moonlit sky and sighed. "I be well, Bishop."

"*Gut* . . . *gut* . . . and the young married couple? They are as fine as flour, *jah*?"

Abner resisted the impulse to roll his eyes. "*Jah*," he rapped out clearly.

"And you and Anke, you make your own cake, *jah*? Chocolate, I think, with peanut butter icing?"

Abner stared into the *auld* man's dark eyes. *What was the bishop asking? How en der weldt could the man suspect anything about his feelings for Anke?*

"I'm sorry, Bishop Kore. I'm going home ta bed. . . ."

"Of course you are, Abner. Don't mind me. Don't mind me a jot."

"I won't," Abner muttered as he turned away. The bishop had ruined a perfectly *gut* moonlight walk.

Anke had finished the supper dishes and, because she was bored, decided to make fudge. Assembling ingredients for both peanut butter and chocolate peanut butter flavors, she took her heavy-based pot to the sink pump for a bit of a rinse. Glancing out the window into the moonlit grass, she almost jumped as Abner stalked past.

Without thinking, she hurried to the back porch door and thrust it open. "Abner?"

She decided that she'd missed him and felt chagrined with herself for even trying to catch his attention in the first place.

"Anke, is everything all right?"

"Abner! Ya about scared me ta death."

"I'm sorry," he said from the steps of the porch. "I thought I heard ya call."

"Well, I did at that. I'm makin' some fudge, if ya'd like ta *kumme* in." Anke's toes curled in her sturdy shoes as she waited for his answer. She felt about as flighty as a *maedel* on her *rumspringa*.

"*Jah*," he said at last. "I'd like ta *kumme* in."

"*Gut*!" Anke took refuge from her boldness in being brisk.

She swallowed as he passed by her in the doorway. He had the fresh, clean scent of pine soap about him, and his shirt had come unpinned at the collar so that she could see the lean line of his throat.

She hastily dragged away her eyes, realizing that he stood with his hat in his hands, obviously waiting for something to do.

"I'll get the sugar and water going. Have a seat at the table, Abner."

He nodded and pulled out a chair, then sat down, the wood creaking under his big frame.

Conscious that he was watching her, she beat around in her brain for something to say.

"Nice nacht *jah*?" she asked, feeling silly at the simple comment. But it seemed to open up a wellspring of conversation in him.

"*Jah*. Though I ran into Bishop Kore—that man can be *narrisch*. Chocolate cake and peanut butter icing . . . If he wasn't such a wise leader—at church meetings—I don't know what I'd think."

"Chocolate cake? Was he hungry?" Anke asked in confusion. She glanced up from the kettle to see that Abner's handsome face was flushed.

"*Nee*, not hungry," he mumbled. "Forget I said anythin'."

Anke shrugged. "All right. I'll forget it."

Chapter Nine

Tabitha awoke from her nap in the boughs of the maple tree to discover with despair that the pink and purple fingers of dawn were stretching across the sky. She'd overslept! She quickly shimmied down from her perch and bent to stroke the faithful Huntress's thick fur, then set off quickly through the dew-drenched forest. She needed to get to Matthew's tent before he woke.

Matthew had slept rather fitfully during the night, trying to stay alert in case Asa or the others decided to catch him unawares. But toward dawn, he fell into an exhausted sleep and began to dream.

He felt the tender touch of a woman's hands along the sides of his cheeks and then down to the curve of his mouth. Her lips soon traced the path of her hands, intoxicating him with a dandelion wine sweetness that he had never known before with a woman. Her mouth found the line of his throat, and he dreamed that he raised his arms, the better to try to hold this intoxicating vision. . . .

But then he woke, his body wet with sweat and his

mind in a tumult over the very vivid dream he'd had. He heard the other men begin to wake and he soon joined them for breakfast, laying aside his thoughts in favor of the day's work ahead.

Tabitha had slipped from her husband's tent and made it back to the safety of the deeper forest before any of the men awoke. With Huntress beside her, she allowed herself to revisit the minutes in the tent with Matthew. In truth, she had expected it to be difficult to figure out how to kiss him. She'd never kissed any man save her *fater*, though many of her would-be betrothed suitors had tried . . . and failed. *Nee*, she had to admit that kissing Matthew had been pleasurable, and by the way his breathing had changed and he'd returned her kisses, she felt that he too had found enjoyment in her effort.

Still, she was no closer to having the marriage consummated, and she had to admit that sneaking kisses along his strong throat still didn't count for much—except perhaps that she was thinking about the consummation as being something more than a moment to get past.

Now she waited as the camp of men woke up and, for some reason, felt led in her spirit to stay and watch the work of the harvesting of the red oak.

Matthew swung the double-bitted ax with ruthless precision. He knew that he was being tested by the men, who wanted to gauge his strength and knowledge of hard work. He didn't mind; he knew he could swing an ax all day if necessary. As it was, he'd been working alone for close to two hours. Even Big Jim must've known that this was Matthew's fight because he didn't try to interfere.

Matthew had just about finished when a storm came up without warning, roaring down the hollow with lethal force. Matthew was conscious of the ominous creaking of the tall tree he was felling and called for the men to run. Although he'd notched a proper hinge in the tree to control its fall, the wind meant that all bets were off as to where the tree would *kumme* down.

Matthew had dropped the ax and started to run when he saw Big Jim lose his footing. He paused for an instant to help the other man to his feet, but just then a terrifying crack split the air. Matthew suddenly felt as though everything was moving in slow motion. He saw the old oak tree come crashing through the tree cover and get hung up for a moment in the limbs of another tree. *Widow-maker* . . . the words pulsed through his consciousness just as the oak broke free and started to finish its descent. He couldn't seem to get his footing and he thought briefly of Tabitha, sure that he was about to die there in the forest. Then he felt something hit him hard in the chest, knocking him clear—a blur of gray fur and wide, sapphire-blue eyes played in racing images before him until a sickening thud echoed in his brain, and everything sank into darkness. . . .

Tabitha sucked in her breath in harsh gasps as she rolled free of Matthew in the pouring rain. She frantically crawled back to him and ran her fingers through his hair, finally settling on the large knot from the rock he'd hit. Huntress whined beside her as Tabitha struggled to think what to do. The men might care for Matthew but be sloppy about it. Yet if she revealed herself, they would likely feel that her husband was weak if he needed to be rescued by the hands of a woman.

Big Jim's shout made up her mind for her, and she grabbed Huntress's collar and got to her feet to dash back into the forest under cover of the pounding rain. She watched from the bushes as Big Jim crawled through the leafy branches to the place where Matthew lay in a fast-growing puddle of rain.

She could see that Big Jim wasted little time hefting Matthew over his shoulder and working his way back to where the other men waited. Then Tabitha spoke softly to the wolf dog, and they turned in unison to begin their journey back to Aenti Fern's cabin while the storm passed over as quickly as it had *kumme* through.

Matthew was vaguely aware that he was being dragged through the woods on a stretcher of some sort, but his head hurt too badly for him to care, and he drifted back into the comfort of unconsciousness.

Chapter Ten

"What happened?" Abner bent near the stretcher with a grim expression. The buwe was sickly pale and seemed to have a fever of sorts.

Abner listened to the explanations and the far-fetched tale of a ghostly *Amisch buwe* who'd saved Matthew from certain death by pushing him out of the way of the oak.

"A ghost *buwe*, huh?" Abner knew the men's penchant for the supernatural, but he also knew Tabitha. "Get him up ta Aenti Fern's and I'll *geh* along with y'uns."

Once there, Abner hoisted Matthew to his feet and dragged him inside Aenti Fern's cabin. Tabitha hurried across the pegged floor to greet them, displaying no surprise at the arrival of her ailing husband.

"Take him in ta the bed, Abner. We'll be fine from there," Aenti Fern instructed.

"*Jah*, but I'm not fine," Abner grumbled, giving Tabitha an arch look.

But after Abner laid Matthew down carefully, the young wife was only focused on her *mann*.

Abner gave up on Tabitha for the moment and went

back into the adjoining room, where Aenti Fern was grinding something with a mortar and pestle.

"Was Tabitha here for the past two days?" he asked abruptly.

"Define here." Aenti Ruth smiled.

Abner sputtered. "Here . . . in this cabin!"

Aenti Fern considered. "You know what the *Englisch* say, dontcha? 'What goes on in the cabin, stays in the cabin. . . .'"

"Ach, may heaven spare me from *auld* and young women alike!" Abner groaned, then left the cabin with a quick slam of the door.

Tabitha sought the hook-and-eye closures of her husband's wet shirt and bent to speak softly in his ear. "Matthew? It's me, Tabitha. . . . You're going to be all right. . . ."

She was surprised to see his eyelids flutter; he groaned faintly. It seemed an instinctive thing for her to bend and carefully press her mouth to his in a soft kiss. And, just as it had at the campsite, his response to her sent tiny shivers of pleasure coursing through her veins.

"Better medicine than I can give him." Aenti Fern laughed as she entered the bedroom carrying a bowl and a poultice.

Tabitha felt a blush stain her cheeks and wasn't sure how to respond.

"Ach, I've known ya since ya were in wee skirts, *mei maedel*. Do you think I'm too *auld* to remember what it is to be in love or to love someone?"

Tabitha stared at her. "Is there a difference between the two?"

"As different as a frog is from a toad."

"And is he my handsome prince?" Tabitha asked reflectively, reaching to brush Matthew's hair off his forehead.

"That . . ." Aenti Ruth handed her the bowl. "Is for y'uns alone ta figure out."

"Tabby. I haven't been this concerned about someone since your moth—for quite a while." John Stolfus caught his *dochder*'s hand in his own. "How is the *buwe*?"

"He's improving every hour, I believe, Da. He will get well."

"Ach, I should have gone myself to cut the oak! When I think of so suddenly having a *sohn* and just as quickly losing him. . . . Well, praise *Gott* for the ghost or angel or whatever it was that saved Matthew's life."

Tabitha didn't reply, yet strangely, she didn't feel as frustrated with her *daed* for calling Matthew a *sohn*. Didn't she herself rejoice over his escaping the tree that might have crushed his big body to the earth? It mattered little to her that she herself could have been badly hurt. She only knew that in those moments of the storm, she wanted nothing more than to help him.

"I'd better *geh* and check on him," she murmured.

"*Jah*, of course!" Her *fater* bent and kissed her, and she slipped back inside Aenti Fern's cabin to tend to her husband.

* * *

Matthew fully came back to himself a day later, when he was awakened by the distinctive and pungent smell of dog breath. "What the—"

"Huntress, get down!" He watched Tabitha shoo the big dog away from the bed.

"Is that a gray wolf?" he asked with interest. "Or maybe I'm just hallucinating. . . ."

"It's a wolf dog and I think you're finally going to be well."

He noted the satisfaction in her voice as she adjusted a quilt across his bare chest.

"Finally? Has it been long? I remember the oak . . . and then a storm."

"You fell and hit your head. You've been sick for three days."

He reached up a hand to gently cup her chin, and to his surprise, she didn't shy away. "I remember . . ." He struggled to grasp the thought that eluded him as he stared into her sapphire-blue eyes.

"Likely you remember lots of strange things," she said lightly as she moved from his touch. "You've had quite a fever."

"I suppose. . . . But—"

"Will you take some cold tea? Aenti Fern has a spring right outside."

"And have I met Aenti Fern?"

Tabitha laughed. "*Jah* . . . numerous times. She's off gathering herbs right now, but it was her medicine that brought you through."

"And your nursing?" he asked softly.

She nodded, and he knew a strange satisfaction in his heart.

Chapter Eleven

"It's tradition for the bride and groom to make the rounds and receive wedding gifts together," Tabitha explained over the breakfast table.

"Even for a mail-order groom?" Matthew teased quietly.

They were alone at the table; her *fater* and Anke were already about their work, and despite her *daed*'s eagerness to get Matthew to the mill, even he had to make some leeway for the traditions of the Mountain *Amisch*.

The young couple had only been home from Aenti Fern's for a day, but Matthew insisted that he was fine.

"You're sure you're up to walking? We could take the horses."

"A walk would be great, especially one with you."

Tabitha couldn't contain the blush his comment created—because she knew that he rarely said anything without meaning it.

"I agree with you," she murmured and was pleased to see his smile.

They cleared the table together, then washed the few dishes.

"This will give you a chance to learn something of Blackberry Falls," Tabitha remarked as they started out. "Talking with some of these folks is like going back in time. . . . But remember, they might also seem strange to you."

"Strange is interesting." He shrugged, then caught her hand in his own.

With the intimate touch of his fingers laced through hers, Tabitha felt that they were well and truly married. She was so focused on the gentle sweetness between them that she forgot her usual precautions when they stepped onto Grossmuder Mildred's property.

The report of a rifle shot echoed around them and Tabitha sighed out loud.

"Are we being shot at?" Matthew asked. He pulled her behind him, then crouched to the ground.

"*Jah*, it's just Grossmuder Mildred. She's blind—"

"And she's shooting at us?"

Tabitha giggled in his ear and was surprised when he turned and swiped a quick kiss across her lips.

"I love to hear you laugh," he whispered. "Even when we're being shot at."

Tabitha knew a warm tightening in her belly, like the excitement she felt when spring came to the mountain after winter had passed.

"Who's there?" a strong, elderly voice called out.

"Grossmuder Mildred, it's Tabitha King and my new *mann*, Matthew."

"Ach, well, why didn't ya say so? *Kumme* on up on the porch."

Tabitha allowed Matthew to pull her to her feet and they climbed the small rise that led to the cabin. Bright red and pink rose bushes bloomed on either side of the front stairs, seeming in direct contrast to the tall, black-clad *Amisch* woman whose hair, where it peeked from beneath her *kapp*, was bright silver.

She propped her rifle against the porch railing and reached out both hands. "Now then . . . let me see this *mann* of yours."

Tabitha let Matthew step forward, and Grossmuder Mildred reached up to put her hands on Matthew's face. "Hmm . . . nice cheekbones, deep-set eyes . . . what color be they, Tabitha?"

"Emerald green."

"His lips are firm. Meant for kissin', am I right?"

"*Jah*," Tabitha said, low.

Grossmuder Mildred felt her way down to the span of Matthew's shoulders. "A big man, broad and hearty," she pronounced. "Tabitha, ya won't *geh* long without a babe of his fillin' yer belly."

Matthew coughed and Tabitha felt her face flame.

"Ach, don't mind me." Grossmuder Mildred laughed, clapping her hands against Matthew's chest. "It's only when ye're very *auld* or very young that ya can say what ya like. Right, *buwe*?"

"Right."

Tabitha was pleased to see Matthew smile and reach with tender hands to touch Grossmuder Mildred's shoulders. *My* mann *is both gentle and a gentleman. . . . He would handle a* boppli *nicely. . . .* Once more, she felt the excitement in her belly and wondered what strange bond Matthew was weaving between them. . . .

* * *

Matthew carefully opened the small writing desk that was fitted out with all kinds of compartments and little drawers. Fresh parchment and a quill and ink were also there. "This is very *auld*," he said to Grossmuder Mildred. "I don't know what to say. . . . Surely you want to keep something like this in your family?"

"Ha! And what are ya but *mei* family, *buwe*? You and Tabitha? All the earth is family . . . they jest forget sometimes."

Matthew nodded. "*Jah,* I suppose you are right."

"Of course I am. Now, you two *geh* on over ta Oncle Nutter's and he'll tell ya the legend of Blackberry Falls. Nobody does it as *gut* as him."

"We thank you," Matthew said softly and bent to kiss the aged cheek.

"Ach, now. Save such things fer yer wife!"

"Plenty to *geh* around," he teased, then carefully closed the small desk and picked it up, holding out his other hand to Tabitha.

When they were back on the trail he spoke his thoughts aloud. "How does she manage all alone up there?"

"She's lived there all her life. She's memorized the different spaces, and we all take turns dropping in on her."

"Well, she's remarkable. . . . Now, who is Oncle Nutter?"

His wife laughed. "You'll see. . . ."

Oncle Nutter was in rare form. . . . He had his usual bag of walnuts in his lap and would periodically crack one on his forehead before eating the meat. Tabitha watched Matthew, who, to his credit, didn't blink an eye at the odd behavior.

Oncle Nutter shook hands politely, then settled back in a bentwood rocking chair on the front porch while she and Matthew sat opposite on equally comfortable rockers.

"Now, what I got fer y'uns is a story. That's my wedding gift to ya."

"That's lovely," Tabitha murmured.

"Ya already know this one, Tabitha, but it's *gut* to hear now and then ta remember. . . ."

She nodded, prepared to listen, and saw that Matthew seemed in a similar frame of mind.

"Long ago, when Ole Bull, the famous fiddler, was buildin' his castle on the mountainside west of here, an *Amisch maedel* of the woods fell deeply in love with a Swedish lumberjack. . . ." There was a pause for a nut cracking. "Now, back then, an *Amisch* girl couldn't marry anyone from outside her community, but most especially not an *Englischer*, and a foreigner at that. . . . But they planned ta run away together all the same. And, of course, her *fater* got wind of it somehow and forbade the *maedel* ta *geh*. And I bet ya can tell me what happens from here, can't ya, Matthew?"

"Uh . . . she jumps from the falls, and even now you can hear her cries for her lost love?"

"*Gut* man ya are! But, *nee*, not what happened."

"Oh . . ."

"Nope! The two got married—she left the *Amisch*; he become a travelin' salesman and they had fourteen *kinner*."

Tabitha's shoulders shook with laughter when she saw the bemused expression on Matthew's face.

"Forgive me, but how does that have anything to do with Blackberry Falls?"

"It don't!" Oncle Nutter slapped his knee and cracked a nut. "The true Blackberry Falls legend is some made-up thing about faeries kissing the bushes all about so the blackberries grow thick every year. . . . Ye're supposed ta hear the creatures sing if ya stand behind the falls and are truly in love. . . . Rubbish, I say!"

"Ach, you only say that because you haven't stood back there," Tabitha teased.

"Now, now . . . I wuz young once. I mighta heard something, but the gift of the tale lies in the tradition of storytellin'. So now, Matt, ya can tell yer *kinner* the same or anythin' ya like!"

Tabitha was glad to see that Matthew nodded his head in agreement, but then he put his hand to his temple.

"Matthew?" she asked in sudden concern. "Are you all right?"

"Just a bit of a headache . . . I'm fine."

But Tabitha wasn't convinced, and she excused them both quickly. "*Fater*'s planning a big picnic at the berrying next week to celebrate the wedding. We can get the rest of the gifts then."

"Yeah . . . I think Oncle Nutter gave me a headache as well as a story. . . . How does he do that with those walnuts?"

Chapter Twelve

"There are people here to see you," Tabitha announced to Matthew, who was sitting upright and visibly bored on the Stolfus couch. It had been a struggle to get him to take even one day at home to relax since his headache had returned, and she was glad for the appearance of Big Jim and his family at the front door.

Big Jim's wife, Rose, and their twelve-year-old *dochder*, Christi, were infrequent guests at the Stolfus cabin, and Big Jim looked rather nervous, carrying a fine wooden tool chest. He glanced across the room to where Matthew sat and cleared his throat. "We *kumme* to say a few words to Matt, if we could."

"Of course." Tabitha smiled. "*Sei se gut, kumme* in and sit down."

Rose and Christi perched on the edge of a carved-backed love seat while Jim hunkered down next to Matthew on the couch. Tabitha sat down in a black, walnut rocking chair.

"See, it's like this. I told my *frau* that I most likely wouldn't be here if it weren't fer ya, Matt. We wanted ta say *danki* and give you this tool box, seein' as how ye're gonna be down at the mill."

Tabitha watched with secret pride as Matthew accepted the finely carved box.

"*Danki*," he said, reaching out to shake Big Jim's hand. "I'll use it often and be glad to fill it as I get working."

"Well, I stocked it up pretty *gut*. I went down to Cubby's and put a few tools in that ya should have ta start. There's a socket and firm chisel, an auger, a gimlet, and a gauge. And then ya got yer square, compass, hammer, and mallet. Ach, and a nice level too."

"*Danki* again," Matthew said, balancing the box on his legs. "This makes me feel real welcome."

Tabitha smiled at the guests. "Rose and Christi, would you like to join me for some tea with Anke in the kitchen? Then these two can talk about the mill and the red oak."

Rose quickly nodded her assent, but Tabitha was surprised when Christi burst out, "Ach, *sei se gut*, Mamm. Can I sit with Daed and hear about the wood?"

Tabitha was amazed at the question, and her heart went out to the young *maedel*. Before Rose could protest, Tabitha spoke up clearly.

"What a *wunderbaar* idea! You have a special *dochder*." Tabitha swallowed. "When I was Christi's age, I too loved to hear about the wood. Please, Rose, let her stay."

Rose nodded, but was clearly bewildered by her *dochder*'s request, yet Tabitha saw that Matthew's eyes rested kindly on Christi.

Tabitha bit her lip, then turned to lead Rose to the kitchen.

* * *

Matthew was nothing if not observant. And he hadn't missed the surprised tension on Tabitha's beautiful face when Christi had asked to stay. He had a sudden insight into what it must be like to be a woman growing up with a *fater* who yearned only for a *sohn*. And what it was to be female in a community dominated by wood and its working . . . men's work surely. And yet Big Jim included his *dochder* easily in their talk, something Matthew thought Herr Stolfus might not have done for Tabitha.

Matthew came back to the moment when Big Jim mentioned the ghost.

"Fast as lightning, that *buwe* ghost knocked ya outta the way. It was a pure miracle, I say. I've told Rose and Christi too."

"A ghost, you say." Matthew smiled at the excited expression on the young girl's face. Clearly, Christi wanted to add her two cents to the tale.

"*Jah*, Herr King. Daed said the red oak would surely have broken ya in two if it weren't fer the ghost."

"Well, Christi—Big Jim, I'm afraid I remember very little of the whole thing—just that the storm came up fast."

"Ya helped me up." Big Jim suddenly took out a large, red handkerchief and blew his nose prodigiously. "And I won't ferget that. You saved my life."

"I'm glad I was there. Sometimes, I think that *Gott* puts us in difficult situations just so we can help someone else for a moment," Matthew said reflectively.

"That be so." Big Jim nodded. "Now, I'll tell ya about the oak. We peeled the bark right there after we got ya fixed up comfortable behind yer horse. Then we put on the hooks and the horses pulled it through the forest. Took three of the strongest geldings ta git it through. 'Course ya was out of it when we made it ta the mill. Thought *auld* Abner wuz gonna wring somebody's neck when he saw ya wuz hurt."

"Really?" Matthew asked in surprise.

"Really." Big Jim nodded. "Now that we got the red oak, ya can learn how ta make fine pieces with it."

"I like the bowls best," Christi chimed in, and Matthew looked at the girl in surprise once more. "The grain is really close together on a red oak."

"I guess your Daed here teaches you a lot about lumber and woodworking," Matthew said.

"*Jah*, but I can't do no woodworkin'. It's not allowed fer girls. But I can help Abigail Mast with her pottery— that's almost as *gut*."

Matthew nodded. "Pottery can be difficult to do, and I suppose it is deeply valued here."

Christi smiled, but there was a wistful expression on the girl's face that somehow reminded him of his wife. . . .

Chapter Thirteen

"Work tomorrow." Matthew couldn't hide the excitement in his voice.

"*Jah*. I know," Tabitha said drily as she threw her blue dress over the clothes screen in her room. It had been especially hot that late afternoon when Big Jim and his family had gone home, and she was glad for the chance to unwind.

She stepped out from behind the screen, wearing only a brief shift, and quickly clambered between the cool cotton sheets of the bed. She turned on her side and regarded her husband, who was wandering about the room while he undid his shirt.

"What are you thinking of besides work?" she asked finally.

"Hmm? Ach, nothing. I guess I am really tired. My head is starting to ache."

She sat up quickly and patted the side of the bed next to her. "Then *kumme*. Let me rub your temples."

She realized that he looked at her fully then and, almost cautiously, came to sit beside her.

She watched his throat work when she got to her

knees beside him and reached to make tender circles at his temples.

"I'm sleeping on the floor," he said abruptly.

Tabitha didn't break the gentle movement of her hands. "That's fine," she whispered.

He nodded, almost to himself, and she hid a secret smile. She hoped he wouldn't suspect her new ploy of approaching him with a casual air. After a few minutes, when she recognized that his breathing had changed, she casually let her hands trail down his throat and move across his bare chest. Then she pulled away.

She scooped up a pillow and a quilt, then dropped them neatly on the floor. "*Gut nacht, mei mann,*" she said, rolling away from him.

He got up, seemingly dazed for the moment as he dropped to the floor. "*Gut nacht,*" he answered. But she was pleased to hear him toss and turn before she fell asleep herself.

Matthew punched the pillow for the third time as the quiet seemed to roar in his ears. He rolled over and pressed his body into the quilt, glad for the hard counterpressure of the wood beneath. He very much wanted to climb into the big bed above him and make love to his wife. . . . *But all of my jabber about us needing to talk first suddenly feels stupid, because she seems uninterested. . . .* He sighed out loud, then told himself that he was to start at the mill the next day. . . . It was his dream, but somehow it didn't seem as satisfying now as the moments when his young wife touched him. . . .

* * *

Anke finished the chores in the kitchen, then grabbed a lantern from the back porch and the bundle of *nacht* clothes she'd made ready. She walked barefoot to the wooden steps built into the back-creek embankment and sighed with pleasure when her toes touched the cold water.

"Nice out, ain't it?"

"Abner!" she shrieked. "You almost scared me to death!" She swung the lantern in the direction his voice had *kumme* from, then hastily pulled it back when she realized he was in the creek, and bare-chested at that. "I'm goin' back ta the *haus*," she harrumphed.

Then his voice came from the dark—slow and easy. "It's up ta you, but I won't bother ya none. Of course, if ye're nervous of me, I can understand."

"Nervous?" she snapped. "Of you? Ha!" She set down the lantern on a step with a thump.

"If ya like, I'll turn 'round while ya git in," he offered.

"There's no need," she said with a sniff. "I'll just *kumme* in in my dress."

"Suit yerself."

Anke secretly wished she might be bold enough to change into her oversize shift, but she did not want to risk exposing herself to the eyes of any man—let alone Abner.

Chapter Fourteen

Tabitha saw Matthew off to the mill and then returned to the kitchen, feeling at loose ends. Abner sat drinking a cup of coffee while Anke folded tea towels.

"Well, *kind*, it won't be long until ya have yer own cabin and will be workin' fer yer husband," Anke observed.

"*Jah*," Tabitha agreed slowly. In truth, she hadn't thought as far as Matthew and her moving to their own cabin. She'd been so focused on marrying on her own terms that she'd neglected to think what that marriage might mean in reality.

"And Abner, ye'll soon have ta find somethin' else ta occupy yer time," Anke said. "Unless ya plan on baby-sittin' Tabby's *kinner*."

Both Tabitha and Abner turned to stare at Anke, but Tabitha found her voice first. "I think I need some time outside. I'll *geh* and see Abigail up at the pottery shop."

Abner made as if to get up, but Tabitha waved him back into his seat. "*Nee*, Abner. . . . Anke's right. As a married woman, I no longer have as much kidnapping value as I did when I was the sole heir."

"Well, that ain't true," Abner protested, but Tabitha laughed.

"Abner, it's fine. Maybe now you can have a life of your own."

She patted the *aulder* man's shoulder and left the kitchen through the back door.

Abner cleared his throat when Tabitha had gone. "Somethin' ain't right with the girl. I wonder what it could be."

"Ach." Anke shook her head. "She's no longer a *maedel* but a grown woman. Growing up can be sad, I suppose."

"Was it sad for you?" Abner asked in a soft voice. *What am I saying? I sound like a fool. . . .* He was about to wave away his question when he was amazed to see Anke's gentle brown eyes fill with tears.

"I suppose that I—I *kumme* ta that sadness earlier than some do. . . ." she whispered.

Abner found himself on his feet. He moved close to Anke and put a gentle hand on her soft shoulder. "Anke? What is it?"

She shook her head mutely, then moved away from him. "It's nuthin'. I best *geh* get the laundry up." She left the kitchen without looking at him, and he stood, feeling tears sting his own eyes.

Anke stabbed the clothespin onto the flapping sheet and ignored the tears that fell past her mouth. *It's not fair . . .* she sobbed inside. *I should be able to have a husband of my own without always thinking of my oncle. . . .*

He was an evil man, but maybe I'm guilty too . . . After all, I done what he told me. . . .

"Woodwork requires skill, *jah*, but it also needs vision." John Stolfus spoke seriously as he showed Matthew around the mill.

Matthew felt more nervous than he had when he'd gone to harvest the red oak. He nodded to various men he recognized from the trip and even gave Asa Zook, his apparent nemesis, a direct look. He knew he'd have to work with these men and *kumme* to know them, but a mill was a dangerous place. He'd have to be careful while he worked.

He recognized orderly piles of mahogany, birch, pine, cherry, and maple woods. Then they passed the close-grained pieces of red oak, and Matthew caught the distinctive smell of cat urine. Although the red oak was beautiful, there was no getting around the reminder of the cat box when it was freshly debarked.

John led him into his office, a well-kept place except for a drawing board, which held dozens of sketches of furniture and useful objects for the home.

"Sit down, *buwe*," John invited as he closed the door on the noise and bustle of the mill.

Matthew sat down in the chair opposite the mammoth, carved desk. It seemed a vast space from which John Stolfus obviously ran his business.

"We know the quality of the wood by smelling it, *jah*. But also we touch it, we feel it. The wood holds a secret . . . it knows how to be, to become. Working with it is a sensual act; a mysterious and sacred appreciation of what *Gott* has created. We do not worship the tree, but Him Who made the tree—which provides us our purpose-ful work in life."

"*Jah*, sir," Matthew replied, drinking in the words. John's obvious love of his trade made Matthew wonder vaguely what kept his *fater*-in-law from allowing women or *maedels* like Christi to do woodworking. But perhaps it was Bishop Kore himself who would not permit it. . . .

John broke into his thoughts by placing a *gut*-sized piece of the red oak on the desktop in front of Matthew. "I know you have your tools, *buwe*, from Big Jim, and I want you to use them. Take this wood. Carry it and dis-cover its secret. Then carve what it is to be, after you've praised *Gott* for creating it."

"Okaaay." Matthew picked up the wood. It was heavy even though it had been debarked, and the smell of it was quite offensive. He wondered rather wildly if this was why he'd *kumme* to Blackberry Falls—to listen to psycho-babble about the character of wood. But he would praise *Gott* for it and hope for some more direct instruction in the near future.

Then he thought of Tabitha in her short shift, her tender fingers touching his temples. He hadn't been a mail-order groom for nothing—he had a beautiful wife and a woman to build a future with—he would trust *Gott* with the rest.

Tabitha climbed the fern-strewn embankment to Abi-gail Mast's pottery shop. Abigail was an independent woman who was kind but rarely smiled. Tabitha liked her for her way of telling the truth in a straightforward manner. Although Abigail was several years older than Tabitha, she was still a *gut* friend, and today was her birthday.

When Tabitha arrived Abigail was shaping a large mug on the wheel, which was powered by foot movement. Tabitha watched in fascination, as she always did, while her friend created art. When Abigail got up she went to wash her hands in the sink.

"*Gefeliciteerd!* Happy Birthday!" Tabitha cried when her friend turned back to her.

Abigail nodded. "*Danki*."

"And"—Tabitha reached into her apron pocket—"this is for you!"

Tabitha slid a small, exquisitely carved duck into Abigail's hands. "Ach, Tabby, it is truly beautiful. The cedarwood has such a pretty grain. *Danki*!" She gave Tabitha a brief hug, then turned to place the duck on the mantel, where several other small, carved animals resided.

Then Christi, Big Jim's *dochder*, brought some firewood from the back of the shop and exclaimed in a loud voice, "Ach, you have a new carving!" Her wide, blue eyes grew even wider. "*Frau* King, did you—did you make it?"

Tabitha's eyes rested briefly on the young *maedel*, then flicked to Abigail, who shrugged.

"*Jah*, Christi, I did."

"*Jah*? But you—we ain't allowed."

Tabitha shrugged. "There are many things a person can and cannot do. It's Abigail's birthday and I gave her a gift from my heart, as I've done before."

"You could be shunned," Christi said. "But I won't tell yer secret ta nobody."

"*Danki*, Christi. I appreciate that."

"Do ya think ya could teach me how to carve?"

Tabitha laughed ruefully. "I don't know how I can resist, but if we're ever caught, you must give me your solemn promise that you will let me take the blame."

"Ach . . . I couldn't let ya—"

"Then I won't teach you," Tabitha said firmly.

Christi considered, then spoke solemnly. "I give you my promise."

Tabitha nodded. "Then we have a deal."

Chapter Fifteen

After supper that evening Matthew picked up his wood and was grateful to head to Tabitha's room. He was exhausted emotionally and was lying beneath a quilt on the floor, his wood by his head, before Tabitha even came upstairs.

He was half asleep when she came in but roused enough to blink at her in the gentle light from the lantern he'd left glowing on her bedside table. She sat down on the floor next to him and reached out to tap the piece of red oak.

"Smells lovely." She smiled.

"I know." He reached up to gently cup her cheek in his hand. She was so delicately made, yet so strong inside.

"Did Da tell you to carry the wood around until it became something?"

"Have you heard that speech before?"

"Only from him to Abner, never to me."

Matthew frowned. "Do you wish he'd said it to you? I mean, the other day with Christi, you seemed—"

"I don't want to talk about this," she said, her easy manner disappearing as she got to her feet.

"All right," he said levelly. He was too tired to figure out why she reacted the way she did whenever he tried to get too close. *But maybe that's it*, he thought. *She barely knows me and I'm expecting her to be completely honest. . . . I certainly haven't been, especially about the reason I answered her ad. . . .*

"It's a dough bowl," she said from above him. She was leaning her head over the edge of the mattress.

"What?" He laughed as her hair tickled his face.

"Your wood. I see a dough bowl."

"Then a dough bowl it is, my sweet! Just for you."

"For us," she reminded him.

"*Jah*, for us."

The next day dawned clear and bright—the perfect weather for the blackberry frolic the community had planned. Her *fater* had declared a Friday holiday from the mill and she felt excited to spend the day in her husband's company. Tabitha dressed quickly in a lavender dress and spotless apron and *kapp*. She couldn't resist stooping down and brushing her lips across Matthew's while he still slept.

She was surprised when he opened his green eyes and toppled her over onto his bare chest.

"I dreamed that a beautiful *maedel* was kissing me awake, and I see that my dream is real." His voice was full of sleep and desire and heat, and she struggled to get up. "Ach, not so fast, my beauty. The price of your release is one more kiss."

She wiggled against him. "We have to get up."

"One kiss," he whispered.

She bent to brush his lips with her own.

"*Nee*," he smiled. "That's hardly a kiss."

She couldn't resist pouting at him, but she knew her eyes sparkled.

"Maybe that was the best you can do." He sighed.

Tabitha knew he was teasing, but something in her rose to the challenge, and she let herself lie full against him, then bent her head until there was but a breath between them.

She blew on his lips as if to awaken them to what was coming, then closed her eyes and ran the tip of her tongue over his bottom lip, again and again, until she felt his breathing and body change. She pressed her mouth to his and squeaked aloud when he suddenly rolled over and she found herself pinned beneath him.

She gazed up into the emerald eyes bent so warmly upon her and saw that his pupils were enormous. His clever fingers found the hairpins that held her *kapp* in place and gently pulled it free, spilling her long hair between them.

"I've changed my price," he said with a faintly wicked smile. "I want—"

"Tabitha! Be ya comin'?" It was Anke, knocking loudly on the door. "We'll be late!"

Matthew buried his head in Tabitha's neck. "I'd like to be late," he muttered. But then he lifted his head and carefully got to his feet, pulling her up to stand next to him.

"*Jah*, Anke!" Tabitha called. "I must fix my hair. That's all."

"Well, hurry on!"

Tabitha looked up into his handsome face. "We must hurry on," she whispered, leaning against him.

He bent to kiss her once more.

And she smiled.

Anke was glad once Tabitha and Matthew had clambered into the back of the hay-filled wagon. John and Abner were up front driving, and she situated herself comfortably on a hay pile.

"Well, Matthew," Anke said, feeling the spirit of the day, "what do ya know about black caps?"

"Black caps . . . you mean blackberries?"

"Ach, so ya do know a bit!"

Matthew smiled at her. "*Jah*, a bit, but I bet you could tell me more. I've heard that during the Civil War, men from opposing sides would declare temporary truces so they could both forage for the berries and make tea out of them to ward off disease."

"Ach, I don't know much about war, except that our people helped with the Underground Railroad in various places, but I bet ya didn't know that Blackberry Falls was a sacred place for the Native Americans hereabout."

"They used the berries for special teas as a sign of hospitality from one tribe to another," Tabitha chimed in.

"*Jah, kind*, right ya are, and we must be respectful as we take the berries for our use." Anke nodded.

Then she noticed that Abner was glancing back her way from his seat up front, and she felt self-conscious. She reached up a hand to touch the top of her *kapp*, then quickly looked away from his blue eyes when she noticed him smiling at her. It was a strange thing to feel such excitement in her chest, a bubbling stream of expectation. *But what if he knew? What if he knew. . . .*

She arranged her features in an expression she thought suitable for an *auld* maid and did not look his way again. . . .

Chapter Sixteen

Matthew was surprised at the sheer number of *kinner* present at the frolic. His own home in the river valley far away had seemed to be made up mostly of young adults and *aulder* folks. "I can see we have a lot of catching up to do," he teased his wife softly as two twin *buwes* ran giggling past with a pail of blackberries held between them.

"Do you mean the berries or the *kinner*?"

"Both." He bent to kiss her on the cheek, then pulled away when Big Jim and Rose approached.

"Ach, hiya, Matt. Want ta take a shot at the thorny berries at the top of the falls?" Big Jim asked with a smile.

"Don't fall," Rose said anxiously.

"*Jah*," Tabitha joined in. "The rocks can be slippery."

"We'll be right as rain," Big Jim promised, and Matthew nodded as his friend led him off to where the sound of rushing water grew much louder.

High in the uplands of the Endless Mountains, pure water bubbles up through rifts in ancient rock. These are the headwaters of Blackberry Creek, which angles down a good mile to drop over the edge of a fifty-foot cliff—creating Blackberry Falls, with its deep pool at the bottom. Here, wildflowers, ferns, mosses, and thorny blackberries form an embankment that seems almost enchanted with mist from the falls.

Matthew could see, as they hiked to the top, that there was indeed a smooth rock nook behind the falls themselves. "Have you and Rose heard the faeries sing, Big Jim?"

To his surprise, his friend flushed red. "*Jah* . . . though I suppose it was just an echo of the water itself."

"Uh-huh." Matthew laughed. He looked down at the mossy ground spread out below and automatically sought the trim form of his wife in her lavender dress. Tabitha was talking to Christi, and the girl seemed, even from this distance, to be highly excited about something.

"Hey, Jim?"

"Jah?"

"Why is it that no women are allowed to do woodworking in Blackberry Falls?"

Big Jim stopped abruptly on the trail and turned around to face him. "I'm sorry, Matt. That's not my story to tell."

Matthew squinted into the sun. "I should ask Bishop Kore, then?"

"You might . . ."

"But it's not his to tell either?"

Big Jim turned back around and stretched out a long arm to carefully pick some of the ripe blackberries. He handed a few back to Matthew.

"Can't say, Matt."

"I understand." *But I don't really, and I wish I did for* mei frau*'s sake. . . .*

Abner strolled about with a mug of blackberry mead in his hand. John always put up a few gallons of the sweet drink, and today it had Abner feeling festive and relaxed—so much so that he sought out Anke.

She was cutting huge slices of frosty watermelon and barely glanced up when he approached.

"I'm busy," she muttered.

"So I see, but perhaps you might walk with me to see the *kinner* in the creek, and to pick a few blackberries?"

She looked up at him then, and it was all he could do not to lose himself in the gentle depths of her soulful brown eyes. Instead, he reached out his free hand and gently ran a finger down her hot cheek.

She seemed frozen by his simple touch, and he knew a headier sensation than even drinking a gallon of blackberry mead would give him. He watched her wet her lips, and then she carefully put the watermelon piece she held and the knife back into the tub. She rose to her full height, which was little more than to his shoulder, and he offered his hand, palm up. Her fingers had just brushed the pads of his fingertips when a loud voice broke the spell of the moment.

"Aha! So we are serving chocolate cake with peanut butter icing today! Marvelous monkeys and pollywog poop!"

Abner turned in irritation to see Bishop Kore standing five feet away and longed to wring the *auld* man's neck, no matter how irreverent the act might be.

"Bishop," Abner muttered in greeting.

When he turned back around he discovered that Anke had gone. He saw her with a group of other women who were setting out food on a long picnic table. *She's hiding. . . .* Abner blinked and peered suspiciously into his mug. It didn't seem to be his thought, but he knew it was the truth—Anke was hiding! The realization gave him a sudden perspective about her that he'd lacked before. He knew then that it would take patience and time for Anke to trust him and to reveal her true self—a woman he'd only caught glimpses of, a woman who left him yearning for more.

"What were you and Christi talking about? I noticed that she seemed quite excited," Matthew asked as he and Tabitha went to look at their wedding gifts.

"Nothing much. She probably looked upset because of the heat. I think she gets very red," Tabitha murmured, then quickly caught his hand in hers. "Ach, look Matthew, a new saddle!"

She knew that she was lying but couldn't bring herself to tell him the truth, and she hoped that the distraction of the wedding gifts would turn his attention.

"Here, then," Oncle Nutter said, coming over to them. "Here's another gift for ya both."

He handed them a brown paper bag, and Tabitha shook it playfully. "Nuts?"

"Black walnuts, and mind that ya remember ta wear gloves when ye're takin' off the hulls. Nuthin' stains like black walnuts."

He cracked a nut from his own, smaller bag on his

forehead and wandered off, leaving Elam Smucker and his mother to approach with their gift.

"Ah." Matthew bent low to whisper in her ear. "Your would-be defender."

Tabitha smiled up at him briefly, then lightly slapped his arm.

"I hope all is well, Tabitha," Elam said, giving Matthew a disdainful look.

"Why, *jah*, of course," she murmured, sliding her arm through her husband's.

"Elam, *gut* fellow." Matthew nodded to the other man. "You would have defended the honor of my wife, even from me. I appreciate that."

Elam sniffed and his *mamm* bristled. "What's this about?"

"Nothing." Tabitha smiled with *gut* grace. "I'd like you to meet my husband, *Frau* Smucker. Matthew King."

"*Jah*, I've heard. Here is your gift. I'll tell you now that it's a set of pink doilies—hand-crocheted of course."

"I like pink," Matthew said succinctly. "*Danki.*"

Anke carried around a tray of blackberry crisp for folks to try. Everyone's recipe was just a bit different, and Anke was grateful for the murmurs of appreciation she got after the first bite. But she couldn't put from her mind the moment that she very nearly took Abner's outstretched hand. W*hat is wrong with me? I am too* auld *to be even thinkin' of holdin' a man's hand—and in public too. . . .*

She was so absorbed in her own thoughts that she failed to notice the first plops of rain hitting her metal tray. Then she heard the noise of the *kinner*'s joyful screams as they danced in the rapidly falling rain. She was turning to run to the shelter of the nearby trees when Abner caught her arm and tugged her toward the falls.

In seconds, it seemed, they were across the wet stones and had entered the relatively dry space behind the falls. Anke drew in deep breaths and reached with one hand to wipe her wet face while balancing her tray against her belly.

Then she looked up into Abner's face, and the intensity of his blue eyes in the filtered light seemed to hold her spellbound. She swallowed hard and felt a thrill of some unknown sensation race down her back. "Wo—would ya like some blackberry crisp?"

Abner smiled and shook his head. "*Nee*."

She watched in fascination as he bent his long back and tilted his head down close to her.

"*Nee*, but I'll take a sweet just the same."

And then he kissed her, his mouth firm, intent. She hesitantly kissed him back and felt his lean fingers grip her shoulders, the wet tray between them. Somewhere, from the back of her mind, the sound of singing seemed to mix with a bridal veil of mist around them, and she longed to stand there forever with him.

But then, fear and anxiety rose up like a wellspring within her and she backed away from him. She heard the low groan that was wrung from him and wanted to *geh* back and soothe his mouth with hers once more, but she couldn't . . .

"Anke?" he whispered as he lowered his hands from her shoulders.

She shook her head and drew in a sobbing breath.

"Abner . . . *sei se gut*, ya can't—we can't ever do such a thing again."

"But . . . why?"

"We can't," she said. "We never can." She pushed past him with her tray and went back out into the rain.

Chapter Seventeen

As the heavy rain continued, the blackberry frolic was moved to the Stolfus cabin. The large place easily accommodated those of the community who chose to attend, and the wedding gifts were dried and put on display in the comfortable living room.

Matthew had gone upstairs to Tabitha's room to change his soaked shirt. He went to the bottom drawer of the large maple dresser where Tabitha had put away the few shirts he'd brought in his backpack. When he'd searched through a handful of Tabitha's shifts, he decided that he had the wrong drawer. He decided to try the next one up and found one of his shirts, but something at the side of the drawer caught his eye. He reached down and pulled out a magnificently hand-carved ladle of hardwood.

Obviously tooled by a master craftsman, the bowl of the ladle and the handle were all of one piece. He turned it slowly in his hands, feeling its balance and admiring the waxed grain of the wood. He'd just put it back, wondering who'd made it for Tabitha, when the creak of the door opening made him look up.

A girl stood there with a smile playing about her pretty

mouth. She looked about nineteen, and Matthew didn't like the predatory glare of her green eyes.

"Uh, I think you have the wrong room," he said, rising to hastily pull on his shirt.

"Ach, I don't think so. I'm Amy Dienner. And you look very much like the right . . . room."

Matthew sighed. If there was one thing he understood, it was being young and having the expectation that you could have whatever you wanted, if you tried hard enough. . . .

He automatically sought the hook-and-eye closures on his shirt and discovered they weren't there. *Tabitha must have taken them off . . . where are the pins anyway?*

The seconds he hesitated gave Amy Dienner enough time to cross the room and lay her hands flush against his chest.

"Look, Amy . . . this is *mei frau*'s room and . . ."

"*Jah*, her room. But I'd guess not yours together. Tabitha Stolfus is too much of a cold witch to ever give a man like you what you need. Why, I bet she doesn't even—"

"Doesn't even what, Amy?" Tabitha's strident voice whipped across the room, and Matthew took an automatic step away from the other girl. "What exactly don't I do for *mei* husband? I suggest you *geh* home and consider your childish words or . . . try to find your own *mann*. I can tell you, though, that little sneaks with mean mouths rarely get what they want because they're never happy with what they have."

Matthew watched Amy flounce back across the room and sidle past Tabitha as if she was a wild cougar. The door slammed behind her and Tabitha met his gaze with glittering, sapphire-blue eyes.

"Amy Dienner? She's all of nineteen. . . . Is that what you want in a woman?"

He sighed, glancing at the dresser top. *Where were the pins . . .* "Tabitha, she came in while I was changing my shirt—that's all."

"And yet she somehow found a way to get her hands on your bare skin."

He shook his head. "She's young; it meant nothing."

"You know, I never have considered what your personal experiences have been with other women back home. Perhaps that is something we can talk about tonight while you are sleeping on the floor?"

She whirled away and flung open the door, only to slam it behind her again.

"Spitfire," Matthew said with a smile when she'd gone. "Beautiful little spitfire."

Abner had sought the refuge of his small cabin after the frolic moved to the Stolfus *haus*. He had no desire to see Anke at the moment, though he could still feel his mouth burn from the heat of kissing her.

He had no idea what was going on with Anke and he suddenly felt very *auld* and tired—too tired to consider the labyrinth of a woman's mind. He leaned back in his comfortable chair near the woodstove and was about to have some more blackberry mead when there was a quick knock on his door.

For one moment he thought hopefully that it might be Anke but then dismissed the idea as being foolish.

"*Kumme* in!" he called.

He was surprised and not a little concerned when Tabitha slipped inside. His charge looked ruffled, as if she'd had a *gut* tussle with someone. There was a hectic color in her cheeks and golden-blond tendrils escaped her *kapp* to fall on the shoulders of her damp dress.

"You're goin' ta catch pneumonia," he observed. "Why didn't ya change?"

She sighed and sat down in a chair opposite him. She'd sat in the same spot many times when she'd had some problem to work out or some secret to confide that she didn't want her *fater* to know.

"I didn't change because I caught a girl in *mei* room with *mei* husband, and he didn't seem to be protesting all that much."

"What?" Abner choked on a swallow of mead.

"*Jah* . . . well, it's true that he wasn't the one touching her, and I did take all of the hook-and-eye closures out of his shirt . . ."

"Was the *buwe*, uh . . . dressed?" Abner trailed off, uncertain as to how to proceed short of giving Matthew a *gut* shake.

"Of course he was. . . . *Nee*, I probably reacted a bit too fast. . . . Why are you sitting all alone here in your cabin?"

He blinked as he tried to adjust to the change of topic. "I—I'm a bit tired. That's all."

She looked at him carefully, and he wanted to squirm in his chair. The child always had had a way of seeing right through him. . . .

"Poor, dear Abner. I suppose that I've led you a merry

chase these past years, and I've never said how grateful I am to you for fetching Matthew here."

He almost sighed in relief. "It was my pleasure, *kind*. I wanted ta see ya married and happy."

"Well," she said meditatively, "I guess I've discovered that planning to marry and actually being married—really understanding and knowing Matthew—are two different things." She smiled. "But I think it will be worth it in the end."

Abner took a long pull of his mead and nodded in agreement, glad that any mention of Anke had been avoided.

Late that *nacht* Matthew lay on his quilt on the floor, staring up at the beamed ceiling while listening to his wife get settled in bed. Suddenly, she spoke from above him, and he thought sleepily that even her voice seemed beautiful in the quiet darkness.

"So," she said with obvious interest. "Tell me."

"Tell you what?"

"About your women—back home."

He laughed and flung his arm over his eyes. "I didn't have any women."

"You did," she insisted. "Unless I will be the first you'll ever—"

"You don't need to finish that thought."

"Aha! So, I'm right, aren't I?"

"You're not going to let this *geh*, are you?" he asked.

"*Nee*," she said, and he heard the steel in her tone.

"Ach, what do you want to know?"

"Everything."

"Like what?"

"Who was the first woman you . . . ach . . . made love to?"

He shook his head against his pillow. *There is* nee *way that this can turn out* gut. "It was a long time ago."

"How long?" she demanded.

He gave in to an impulse and got to his knees at the side of the bed. Tabitha lay still, watching him. He reached out a hand to trail down the gentle curve of her throat, twining her honey-gold hair about his fingers. Then he looked into her eyes. "It was during my *rumspringa*."

"Oh." Her pink lips parted.

He nodded, then loosed her hair to continue trailing his finger downward to the deep valley between her breasts. "She was *Englisch*. An *aulder* woman if you must know."

"I must know," she whispered, and he could feel her breathing change, becoming more erratic as he traced with tender fingers the upward slope of one breast and then the other, going back and forth.

"She taught me how to kiss, how to touch, what to do. . . ."

By now Tabitha moved restlessly beneath his touch, but after a moment more, she looked at him and gave a slight nod. "I understand and am glad to be the beneficiary of your—experience."

"Anytime, sweet." He gave her what he knew to be a lopsided grin, finding himself painfully caught in his own sensual web. "Anytime."

Chapter Eighteen

Anke finished the breakfast dishes while Tabitha dried the blackberries that had been picked in the rain the day before. She set them out carefully on long, white tea towels and picked out any hulls. Blackberries could turn soft very easily and had to be treated with care.

As she turned the berries, Tabitha thought of her husband's touch the *nacht* before. She felt herself blush when she thought of how caught up she had become in the sound and the spell of his voice.

"Are ya dryin' those berries or feelin' 'em ta death?" Anke's voice broke into Tabitha's thoughts, and she hastily refocused on her task.

"I'd like to churn some fresh ice cream tonight for dessert and make blackberry-vinegar caramel sauce for Matthew to try."

"Hmm . . . if ya like." The sheer lack of enthusiasm that Anke displayed in Tabitha's rare interest in food caused the younger *maedel* to look at her friend in surprise.

"Anke? Are you all right?"

"Of course, I am." But, as if to disprove this statement,

Anke dropped the butter crock as she turned to the table, and it shattered with a crash.

To Tabitha's surprise, Anke began to cry, something she'd never seen her do before.

"Here—" Tabitha knelt with a towel to where Anke had slid down next to the splat of butter and shards of crockery. "You're going to cut yourself, Anke. Let me clean it up."

"Ya can't," Anke wailed. "No one can clean it up."

Tabitha put her arm around her friend's shaking shoulders. "Please don't cry, Anke. It's all right."

But it was a long while before Anke's sobs died away and Tabitha was able to begin on the blackberries.

Matthew watched Big Jim expertly turn the lathe in the center of the green butternut wood in preparation for hollowing out a dough bowl. Matthew was to follow, in theory, with the piece of red oak Tabitha had pronounced a dough bowl.

A dough bowl was used for bread making. Once the ingredients were mixed and kneaded in the bowl, the dough was covered with a kitchen cloth and left to do its rising. Wooden bowls held the heat created by the fermentation of the yeast.

Big Jim paused in his carving to eye Matthew's bowl and shook his head. "Mebbe we should've started ya out with buckeye wood—it carves easier."

Matthew rolled his eyes. "I can't seem to get the motion down."

"Takes practice, Matt!" John Stolfus joined the conversation, and Matthew felt himself flush at his *fater*-in-law's words. "Besides, I'd like you to *kumme* into the office, *sohn*."

"*Danki*, Jim, for the training," Matthew said to his friend, then followed John into his office.

"Take a seat, Matt. I actually wanted to tell you that I think you should spend half your time working the wood and the other half learning the business with me. After all, it will be yours to run and guide one day."

"About that—"

"*Nee*, Matt. *Nee* need to thank me. Just the fact that, *Gott* willing, you and Tabitha will soon produce *kinner* is enough to make me want to give you my best hammer!"

"*Jah*, but—"

"So, let me explain the operation side of things to you a bit. We may be remote here in Blackberry Falls, but we run a strong business. Elam Smucker is the post office around here and routinely walks to Farwell, then brings back orders. We get orders from all over and, in fact, I was surprised when Tabby told me that you hadn't heard of Stolfus Lumber and Woodworking, but that's *gut*. I've often worried that some outsider might marry Tabby with an eye to gaining the business and not so much a *frau*."

Matthew sat, miserable at the lie he was perpetrating—not just on his wife but on her *fater* as well. On everyone he'd met in Blackberry Falls—the whole community that had been so kind to him. He sighed inwardly and wanted to begin to tell the truth, but just then, a worker from the mill burst through the door.

"Fire, John! Main shop!"

Matthew jumped to his feet but had to follow his *fater*-in-law, who was around the desk in seconds. They ran to the main shop, where Matthew had been working with Big Jim. The acrid smell of smoke pervaded the air, but the flames had been extinguished. The remains of Matthew's dough bowl made it easy to see where the fire had started. It seemed a clear message of evil intent against him.

John shook his grizzled head, then bellowed out to those workers who were standing by, "Men, a single match can take down our livelihood as well as our lives! I offer a thousand-dollar reward for any information about who started this. Big Jim, did you see anyone pass by?"

"*Nee*, but I had my back turned."

"Well, think on it, men. This was no accident, and the kind of a worker who would do something like this is a danger to us all."

Matthew let his eyes roam over the grim expressions on the men's faces, then thought about Asa's cold words in the dead of *nacht*. Then and there, Matthew promised himself that he would pay a visit to Asa and Micah to see what the *bruders* might be planning.

Tabitha cooked the granulated sugar until it turned a nice, golden brown around the edges. She'd learned the trick of not stirring until the browning occurred, so the caramel wouldn't be ruined. She tapped her foot on the hardwood floor while waiting for the deep, amber color to appear in the pan. As soon as it did, she pulled the pan from the heat and carefully added a tablespoon of vinegar to the caramel. The vinegar caused the mixture to bubble vigorously, then seize. She returned it to the heat and added two handfuls of fresh blackberries to the melting caramel and cooked the whole thing until the berries were softened. She sighed to herself, glad that she'd been able to make the sauce without Anke's help.

Still, she was worried about Anke, who had complained of a bad headache after she'd cried. Tabitha had convinced her to lie down—something that Anke never would have conceded to do normally. Tabitha considered going for Aenti Fern for some headache tea leaves but was distracted by Abner hovering at the kitchen door.

"Abner, whatever are you doing? *Kumme* in!"

Abner slunk in the door and cast his eyes about the kitchen. "Anke's not here?"

Tabitha stared at him. "She's not feeling well. If you'd like, you could *geh* to Aenti Fern's and fetch her some headache medicine."

Abner was back out the screen door with an alacrity that caused Tabitha to wonder if he'd lost his wits. "*Jah*," he snapped. "I'll *geh*."

Tabitha shook her head as she went back to the blackberries, thinking that the world seemed upside down, judging by Anke and Abner's behavior.

Abner set off for Aenti Fern's cabin with hurried steps. He felt his heart pound in his chest. He realized that he was deeply concerned about Anke and feared her being ill. *It's almost as though I love her. . . .* The thought made him nearly trip over an exposed root, and he tried to push the idea away.

He finally gained the path to Aenti Fern's and nearly

burst through the wooden door after only the briefest of knocks.

"Aenti Fern?" he hollered without preamble.

"*Nee*," came a panting voice from the small back room. "It's Mary Lapp. My water broke and I'm gonna have my *boppli*—right now!"

Abner froze, and the unholy desire to back out the door suddenly filled his mind; then Mary groaned and he threw off his hat. He tiptoed to the other room, knocking down herbs and drying flowers from overhead as he went.

"Mary? Where's Aenti Fern?"

The young woman in the bed threw him a desperate glance. "Ach . . . I don't know! I just *kumme* here ta wait and things started happening fast. . . . Accchhhh! You're gonna have to help me, Abner!"

He swallowed and felt as if he'd like to throw up, but he took another step nearer to the bed where Mary was writhing in pain. Her belly looked enormous beneath her blue dress, and he tried once more to make sense of the situation. "Maybe I can find Aenti Fern or some other woman. . . ."

"Abner," she panted. "Noooowwww!"

"All right." He nodded. Then he went to the bowl and pitcher that were on a nearby table and was glad to see a big bar of lye soap. He washed his hands as Mary's cries escalated and tried to think how he might help her. . . . He was mumbling prayers beneath his breath as he dried his hands and then approached the bed.

"Abner, it don't matter that ye're a man . . . I—Ach! You've delivered lambs before, right?"

"Lambs," he muttered. *If only it was a lamb delivery. . . .*

Gott *help me!* "All right, Mary . . . all right now. . . ."
Kumme on, Abner . . . ya can do this!

He lifted the hem of her wrinkled dress with reverent
fear. He could see the crown of the baby's wet head.
"Dark hair, Mary!"

He was almost shouting, and Mary was pushing and
crying, and suddenly, he held a screaming, slippery *boppli
buwe* in his large hands.

"Ach, Mary—he's beautiful!"

"Abner," she cried. "I forgot ta tell ya. . . . Aenti Fern
said it was twins!"

Chapter Nineteen

Matthew entered the Stolfus *haus* alone. John had wanted to keep an eye on the shop, so he'd sent Matthew ahead.

Tabitha took one look at him and must have read the concern he was feeling. She put down a dishcloth and came forward to greet him.

"Matthew, what is it? What's wrong?"

He caught her hands in his and gave her a brief smile. "There was a small fire at the mill."

"What? Where's Fater? Was anyone hurt?"

"*Nee*, no one hurt. But I wanted to tell you, before it gets around, that the fire was set in my sad excuse for a dough bowl."

He watched her pretty brow wrinkle in confusion. He had no desire to worry her, but he felt she deserved the truth—*even if I don't give her truth in other ways.* . . .

"I'm sure it was a beautiful dough bowl," she said finally. But he could see realization dawning in her blue eyes and he gently pulled her close.

She was so small but so very, very strong. It was bad enough that he was bent on finding out whether Asa Zook had had anything to do with the fire; he didn't want Tabitha to try doing the same.

"No worrying, sweet. Now, tell me what smells so *gut*."

Anke paused in the doorway to the kitchen and looked furtively about to see if Abner was there. He wasn't, and she felt both relief and regret. *Perhaps I've scared him off.* . . . She came back to the moment when Tabitha gave her a strong hug.

"Anke, are you feeling better? I've been so worried about you."

"I feel fine now, *kind*. Did the blackberry sauce *kumme* out right?"

"Better than all right," Matthew said appreciatively from the table. "I've never had it before and it's great."

Anke noticed Tabitha blush at the compliment from her *mann*. *Ach, what was it to be so in love, to openly praise each other?*

John Stolfus came through the door at that moment, carrying a batch of fresh-churned ice cream. "Hello, Anke. Are you well?" He put the churn down on the table, and Anke hesitantly took the seat that Tabitha drew out for her.

"*Jah*, John. I be—"

She broke off as Abner suddenly staggered in the door. He looked like he'd been on the losing end of some kind of wild fight. His hat was missing and his hair was awry. His shirt was pulled sideways out of his dark pants and his face was a blank stare of fright. He collapsed into a chair at the table, then buried his face in his hands.

"Abner," Anke cried in alarm, reaching to touch his arm. "What is it?"

He looked up at her then. "Mary Lapp was in labor," he groaned. "Twins . . . Aenti Fern wasn't there. I—I delivered 'em."

There was a moment of silence in the kitchen; then everyone started talking at once. Anke wanted to bury her face in her apron and cry for joy. But instead, she simply squeezed his arm and nodded with a soft smile on her face. Her discomfiture had passed and she wanted to rejoice with him.

John slapped him on the back. "You *auld* dog! Twins?"

"I would have loved to see your face when you were . . . about the business of delivering." Matthew laughed, and Anke saw Abner glare at the *buwe*.

Tabitha gave him a bowl of ice cream and blackberry sauce and stopped to kiss him on the forehead. "You're a *gut* man, Abner."

Anke's heart swelled with pride to hear the kind teasing and praise that was heaped on her friend. . . . *But he kissed me and I heard the singin'. . . . Not just a friend . . . so much more—but that he can never be.*

After supper that *nacht*, while the three men were still talking in the kitchen, Tabitha felt restless and wandered to the small room where all her favorite books were shelved. She idly ran a finger across the spines of the books—some battered and others band box new. She'd loved reading all her life and smiled when she thought of her mail-order groom ad, which had required the prospective applicant to love books.

In truth, she had no idea whether Matthew loved to read, but she knew that she was developing feelings for him that she had never expected. She pulled out *Wuthering Heights* and was thumbing through it when she looked up and saw Matthew standing in the carved wooden doorway.

"Am I interrupting?" he asked in soft tones.

She shook her head and he closed the door behind him and walked toward her. She hugged the book to her chest and watched him move. He had a casual, lithe grace for all his height, and she liked feeling his green eyes on her. He stopped in front of her and bent to place a casual kiss on her parted lips. It left her feeling restless, and she wondered if it was an accident that his lean fingers brushed her breast as he reached to take the book from her. She let it go easily, wondering with excitement what he was about.

He smiled down at her. "Heathcliff? So you prefer a dark and brooding man?"

Nee, her mind whispered, *I prefer a man like you.* She was startled by the sudden thought and half turned away from him.

He seemed to appreciate her posture, though, because she heard the book hit the shelf and then she felt his hands slide up her back to her shoulders. She couldn't control the shiver of expectation that raced down her spine like heated water.

"Mmm," he whispered. "You smell like roses and linen. . . ."

"It's my soap," she choked out.

She felt his breath against the nape of her neck, and then he nipped gently at her left earlobe. She caught her breath and swallowed hard. "Ma—Matthew . . ."

"*Jah*, say my name, sweet, *sei se gut*." His lips brushed the side of her throat and she arched her neck in response, instinctively leaning back against him. She could feel the oaken strength of his chest and the length of his legs pressing her skirts. Thoughts of warm honey spun out in sunshine seemed to fill the back of her mind, and she wanted to share the sweetness with him.

She turned in his arms, facing him, and pressed her hands to his chest, rubbing up and down, and then stretched on tiptoe to kiss him. She imagined that a fire seemed to spark between them, heating the sweetness to flame . . . and then he pulled away.

He put her farther from him and bent to rest his hands on his knees, gasping as if he'd run a mile in high summer wheat. She stared at him, aroused and confused and beginning to feel the fine edges of anger.

"What is your favorite color?" he groaned as he rose once more to his full height.

"What?" she snapped.

"I don't—even know your favorite color. How can I—we . . ."

"That's it!" She pushed past him, intent on leaving the room. "It's blue," she hissed. "But you're going to have to wait a long time to ask me such a personal question again!" She slammed the door behind her and stormed up to her room.

Matthew leaned back against the bookshelf. He hurt—both mentally and physically. But he knew now that until he had told her the truth about the mail-order groom ad, he didn't have the right to fulfill their marriage vows. *Then, at least, she'll have a choice*, he thought. *She can annul the marriage if she chooses. . . .*

Chapter Twenty

Tabitha shifted on the hard, backless bench in church the next day. She hadn't spoken a word to Matthew since last evening and she was amazed to discover that she felt a bit childish in ignoring him. She sighed to herself as she waited for the meeting to begin. It seemed strange to be seated with the married women. Without turning completely around, she couldn't see Matthew. She realized as she reflected that she was used to going her own way and was indeed quick to anger. It was something to work on and pray about, she decided. Especially in light of his kissing, her traitorous mind whispered. . . .

Matthew was only too glad that his wife's slender back was turned away from him. Amy Dienner seemed intent on extending him a personal invitation to the church meeting in her *fater*'s barn. Somehow, the girl had managed to slip through the ranks of married men to where he stood near Big Jim.

"Matthew," she cooed softly. "I'm so sorry we couldn't . . . finish the other *nacht*."

He cleared his throat. Did the girl have no shame? He wanted to roll his eyes, but he also realized that she was playing a dangerous game. He had no desire to put any thoughts of his being an adulterer as well as an outsider into the minds of the men who were chatting close by. But Big Jim seemed to understand the girl's game.

"Amy, *geh* along with ya," Big Jim rumbled. "If ya can't tell, we ain't the young unmarrieds here. . . ."

The girl flounced away, and Matthew breathed an inward sigh of relief. He glanced at Jim. "*Danki.*"

Jim grinned. "There was a time Amy cast her eyes my way. That girl needs to settle down and marry."

Matthew nodded, then turned back to the service, which was just beginning. He was looking forward to seeing Bishop Kore deliver the sermon and wondered if the *auld* leader really seemed normal during his preaching. But first came the singing of the traditional opening hymns from the *Ausbund*, the book of *Amisch* hymns that lacked musical notes. Instead, a male member of the community started off for a few seconds to give the opening note, and then the community followed, with each note lasting as much as four or five seconds.

Soon it was time for the long sermon. Bishop Kore placed his hands behind his back and began to pace slowly back and forth in front of the community. Matthew had the urge to laugh for some reason, imagining that the *auld* man might do anything from a headstand to giving a demonstration of a rhino call.

But Bishop Kore began simply, even elegantly, and Matthew found his attention caught.

"In order to have a successful marriage, *Gott* must be

an ever-present Third in the union. Getting married takes a day. Being married takes a lifetime. A lifetime of discovery, resilience, and persevering faith. For we know that 'Perseverance produces character and character, hope. And hope does not disappoint us, because *Gott* has poured out His love into our hearts through the Holy Spirit, whom He has given us. . . .' And it is His love that makes marriage—that process of ever growing in love, ever enduring in love, ever searching the heart in love, so that we can find new strength to care for one another—possibly, even unto death.

"And let me say also that it is never too late to seek *Gott* and invite Him to become part of your marriage, of your very life. He is waiting for you and loves you very much. Now, I know, as sure as I'm standing here, that there are some gathered who might feel as though *Gott* has deserted them; that He has hurt them, and why would the *Gott* Who is love do such things? I only know that we see the wrong side of the quilt here on earth. We see the under-stitching that a child sees when she runs beneath the quilt frame to find a dropped needle. We see not the top pattern that the Master Quilter sees, those designs and edges, and corners, and tight spots that bring a quilt top to life. So are our lives—we see as small children, but *Gott* knows the eternal design."

Matthew listened in the silence that resounded when the bishop had finished. Never again would he consider Bishop Kore to be beyond odd, because here, when the church was gathered as a body, the *auld* man had the strength and power of *Gott*-given thoughts. . . .

* * *

Tabitha was quiet both in her mind and in her spirit. Bishop Kore's message and simple illustration of being under the quilt had spoken deeply to her. And also, she'd discovered that the idea of marrying Matthew as a lifetime pursuit was something she longed to do. She realized that what he had been saying about getting to know each other was truly a valid and worthy point. As she got to her feet at the end of the service, she searched the gathering for her husband.

She felt a surge of happiness that was hard to explain when he came toward her and she smiled up at him.

"Is that a real smile, *mei* sweet?" he bent to whisper in her ear. "Or is it for the crowd?"

"Real," she said simply, pleased when he smiled in return. She held his arm as they headed out into the sunshine where the community had gathered for the usual picnic that was held after service. They had to pass Asa Zook as he stood in the doorway of the open barn. Tabitha felt strange when he gave her what amounted to an open leer and then decided she had been mistaken when the man turned away.

In any case, Matthew had not seemed to notice, so she let the moment slip from her mind. She realized that now she was married, she was to *geh* and work with the married women, while Matthew went to talk with Big Jim and the other married men. The youth were playing softball and the young *kinner* gamboled after bubbles in the vast expanse of green grass.

Tabitha went to *Frau* Dienner to ask what she might do to help. *Frau* Dienner was a large, kind woman who was absolutely nothing like her *dochder*, Amy.

"Ach, Tabitha, we don't have enough pasta salad for seconds. I don't know what I wuz thinkin'." She gave an exasperated flap to her apron. "Would ya run into the cabin and make up a bowl? All the ingredients are on the table in the kitchen and ya can boil the noodles while ya cut up everythin'."

Tabitha smiled her response and made her way into the cool of the large cabin. It was exceedingly quiet inside and she was glad of the retreat. She put the corkscrew pasta on to boil, then sat down at the long table with a sharp paring knife. She cut up the sharp cheese first, making small, square chunks. Then she started on the cucumbers and tomatoes. She was peeling the onion when she heard the front door open in the next room. She was going to make her presence known when the suppressed sound of feminine giggling came to her. She listened for a moment, not wanting to intrude on anyone, and got up to go to the side of the small archway that led to the living room area. But then she heard Amy Dienner's unmistakable, high-pitched voice.

"Mamm will never know. *Kumme* up ta my room fer a bit of a tumble."

"*Jah*," a man's voice agreed, and then all was silent save for the creaks of the stairs.

Tabitha realized the pot was boiling over, and she hurried to the cookstove to take it off the heat. She cast the noodles into the colander she'd prepared in the sink, then slowly tiptoed back to the table, torn between finishing her assigned task and sneaking outside and away from any trouble Amy was brewing for herself. Tabitha was no prude, but she was shocked that Amy would take such a risk—and in her own *haus*! And who was the man who would agree to such a thing?

Thankfully, though, Tabitha was able to hastily assemble the Italian-spiced dressing and shove everything for the pasta salad into the large wooden bowl. *I'll stir it up outside*, she decided, and then left the kitchen in haste.

Abner felt as though he could barely lift his head without encountering the good-natured smiles of those gathered at the picnic after service. News had spread, as it always did in Blackberry Falls, that he had delivered the twins of Mary Lapp. Lester Lapp, the proud *fater*, had *kumme* to the picnic only to heap more praise on Abner's head.

Lester had caught Abner as he was headed for the sliced ham. "Abner! Abner—what can I say? We're so grateful. Mary and I decided to name the *buwe* after you and the girl after Mary's *mamm*!"

Abner endured the hug of the other man and felt his face flush as he clutched his empty plate to his chest. "*Danki*, Lester," he mumbled.

Folks gathered around them, and congratulations were abundant. But Abner wished the moment would pass as he sidled through the group to the food tables, automatically looking for Anke.

He saw her, down on her knees in the grass, with a willow bubble wand, blowing bubbles from a lid of soapy water for the delighted *kinner* who fluttered about.

She would make a fine mamm. . . . He almost dropped his empty plate at his mind's treacherous reflection. *What would it be to deliver my own* sohn *or* boppli maedel?

This thought had him wondering if he was *narrisch* in the head, but it also propelled him to hastily scoop up a pickled egg. With the beet juice staining the white of his plate, he moved to Anke's side through a curtain of bubbles. He sat down a few feet from her, and she waved the willow wand within inches of his face.

"Ye're gonna spill that egg on ya," she observed.

"Mebbe," he admitted.

The screams of joy from the *kinner* seemed to fade as he caught the fresh scent of Anke's body in the light summer breeze. He felt young for a moment and his mind blurred as he remembered being seventeen and all the pulsing life that ran through his veins—the knowledge that everything lay before him, and no matter how rugged the circumstances, anything seemed possible. . . .

He blinked as a bubble hit his nose and popped. He came crashing back to the moment with an emotional jolt, then swallowed hard. "Did ya play with bubbles when ya were a *maedel*?" he asked Anke.

"*Nee*," she replied flatly.

"Me neither."

"Then ya might as well start now." She got to her feet and waved the bubble wand at him. He took it, and the pickled egg rolled into his lap. When he looked up she was gone.

Matthew was surprised when Big Jim handed him a small, corked brown jug.

"White lightnin', Matt. Always makes the macaroni salad sparkle."

Matthew smiled and took a swig; the liquid burned

like fire in his throat. He handed the jug back to Jim and shook his head. "That's quite a lot of sparkle."

Jim nodded. "Wish I could play softball with the *kinner*. I don't see Christi about, but there goes the bishop."

Matthew turned in time to see Bishop Kore turning cartwheels among the young *kinner* and almost laughed out loud. "How much sparkle has he had?"

"I'd say none," Jim replied. "Usually it's headstands."

Matthew was saved from replying when he saw Tabitha coming from the Dienner cabin, looking flushed and harried.

"Excuse me, Jim. I see *mei frau*." He stepped away from the cluster of men and walked across the grass in time to see Tabitha plunk down a bowl of pasta salad on one of the picnic tables.

"Mad at the salad?" he asked, coming up to stand beside her. Then he looked into her stormy blue eyes. "What's wrong?"

He watched her take a deep breath and then appear to steady herself. She smiled up at him. "Nothing . . . nothing at all."

Matthew shook his head. He wished he knew her better so he could be sure when he read her that he was right. As it was, he had to settle for a plateful of pasta salad and an uneasy feeling that things were not always as they seemed in Blackberry Falls.

Chapter Twenty-One

Anke glanced at Tabitha—the girl seemed preoccupied as they walked the quarter mile to the Fisher General Store, or Cubby's, as it was called.

"What be wrong with you, *kind*?"

Tabitha shook her *kapped* head. "I might ask you the same thing, Anke. You always seem to be thinking hard lately."

Anke sighed inwardly. She had hoped that she'd not given away how much she thought about Abner. It was all foolishness in the first place. . . . "I think about what I always think about," she said finally, unable to lie outright to Tabitha.

The two continued in silence as the bees hummed among the mountain flowers and the sound of the falls lingered in the distance. Anke felt like swinging the basket she held over her arm but decided it seemed too girlish an action. She was glad when Cubby's came into view— a long log cabin with a built-up front porch and wooden steps. Red geraniums burst from two hanging baskets on either side of the steps.

The wide porch was empty, but then, suddenly, the wood-framed screen door burst open and Grace Fisher came out, holding her cheek with one hand. She drew a sudden, sobbing breath when she saw them, then hurried down the steps and ran into the forest.

Anke saw Tabitha make a move as if to follow the other woman and caught her arm. "*Nee, kind*. Don't interfere. Sam Fisher must be drinkin' again."

"What?" Tabitha turned wide eyes to her *aulder* friend. "What are you saying? That Grace Fisher is being . . . hit by her husband? Why haven't I ever known this?"

"Mebbe because ya just now started ta look. Ye'd be surprised at what goes on in this world, *kind*, when everythin' looks fine on top. . . ."

"But now that I know . . . well, we have to do something. Why doesn't she leave?"

"To where, and how?" Anke shook her head bleakly. "It's not so easy a thing. And she has the *kinner* ta think of . . ."

"My *fater* will—"

"Do nuthin'. He's known this goes on fer years. *Nee.* He'll leave it alone. Now, *kumme*, we need our things from the store, and we don't want ta be gossipin' on Grace's doorstep." She led Tabitha to the screen door and propelled the girl inside.

Tabitha angrily grabbed up a five-pound bag of flour from the shelf, disregarding the faint dusting of white that flew in her face. She added sweet pickles and minimarshmallows to her basket, then followed Anke to the counter to pay.

Tabitha let her eyes bore into Sam Fisher's whiskered face, wishing she could will him to look up from the money box and face the accusation in her eyes. But the man went on, calmly pricing things and asking for the total, which Anke drew from the household purse. How could he be such a hypocrite, pretending that all was well? The question plagued her as they left the store. There was no sign of Grace Fisher, and once again Tabitha longed to *geh* and find the other woman, but decided to share the story with Matthew instead.

Matthew turned the wood in his hands, feeling with pleasure the weight and balance of the piece. He ran his thumb down the edge of the shelf and was once more amazed that he had tooled the wood himself. He'd *kumme* to realize that the gentler he was, the better the wood responded. Now he understood what Abner had said about the wood being like a woman, and he felt himself grow hot when he considered whether he might touch Tabitha with the same confident gentleness.

He snapped back to the moment, though when Jim asked him if he would help bring in one of the heavy logs of cedar that were stockpiled under a shelter a hundred feet or so from the mill operation itself. Matthew pulled on his gloves and went outside with his friend. Each man grabbed a hook from the outside wall and went to the log pile to hook the ends of the closest log.

The pile was held in place by peglike stakes at the

base, and it felt good to Matthew to hoist the heavy wood out of its place. But then there was a rumbling sound, and Matthew watched in horrified fascination as the head-high pile of logs began to move. He dropped his end of the log and jumped over it, intending to knock Jim out of the way. Then he realized his mistake as he was caught in the middle of the falling roll of wood. He heard Big Jim's shout and thought briefly of Tabitha's bright smile before he felt an unbearable weight and then everything went dark.

"I tell you, John, one of the pegs that held up that log pile was split." Abner spoke in hoarse tones as they waited outside Aenti Fern's cabin.

"It couldn't have been; it probably happened in the crash. Ach, the poor *buwe*. . . ."

"*Jah*," Abner whispered savagely. "He's blessed to even have a spark of life left in him yet. I'd like ta get my hands on the murderer, because that's what this amounts to—somebody wantin' Matthew dead."

"Don't say that. Besides, it was Big Jim himself who asked for Matt's help and we know how *gut* a friend he is to—"

Abner turned away as the door to the cabin was opened from the inside. Aenti Fern stood there, looking worried. "If I didna think there was a chance we'd hurt him further, I'd say he needs ta be carried ta the hospital in Farwell."

"He needs a doctor then?" Abner asked. "I'll *geh* and git one and bring him back."

"He might not *kumme*," Aenti Fern observed.

Abner gave her a grim smile. "He'll *kumme* all right."

* * *

Matthew drifted in and out of a vast dream forest. He could see great cedars in sunlight and felt as though he need merely touch a tree and it would fall across his path. But he leaped over each log, heading ever deeper into the bright woodlands. The fall of light on the forest floor, rich with wild ferns and blackberries, was enticing. And then he saw the red oak; looking up, he saw it crack—a widow-maker. But someone pushed him out of the way. He knew, somehow, with stark clarity, that the flash of sapphire-blue eyes belonged to his wife and the gray fur was the great wolf dog belonging to Aenti Fern. Tabitha had dived at him like a fury and saved his life. Saved his life . . . but now he couldn't see her, and the call of the glowing forest seemed to lure him. An enticing call . . . but he wanted his wife even more than the light. . . .

Tabitha leaned forward to dab at the cut on Matthew's face—a wicked gash that ran from one high cheekbone to beneath his chin. It was the only injury that she could see, but she knew in her heart that he was badly hurt inside. She moved to shift her weight away from his hip on Aenti Fern's bed, fearing to bump him in case it was his pelvis that was broken. He moaned faintly, and she dipped her cloth into the wooden bowl of water and pressed it to his lips.

She realized in those moments, when spilled blood and broken bone could separate her from Matthew forever, that she had *kumme* to care deeply for him. In truth, she had never felt this way before and she marveled at the awakening that seemed to spread from her mind to her breast. *He is such a* gut *man—so strong and full of truth— it's almost as though I—*

Her thought was lost as Abner banged on the door and entered with a harried-looking *Englischer* in tow.

Chapter Twenty-Two

"Well?" Abner asked brusquely, unwilling to admit to himself how much the *buwe*'s survival meant to him.

"Hmm . . . could be worse, all things considered." The *auld* doctor paused to listen once more to Matthew's lungs with his stethoscope, then straightened his back.

"What does that mean? His *frau* here wants the truth straight." Abner slid his hand to Tabitha's shoulder to brace her for what might be coming.

He had crossed the two-mile trail to Farwell and marched as fast as he could into the small hospital. Nurses had fluttered at him, trying to herd him into the waiting room, but he'd set eyes on the gray-bearded doctor and decided he'd do just fine. If the man hadn't been able to keep pace with him back to Blackberry Falls, Abner felt as though he would have carried him. But they'd gotten there. . . .

Now, Abner waited as the doctor made his pronouncement.

"Broken ribs. Can't do much about those; we don't set them anymore. Right arm broken. I'll put on a cast for that. Concussion. That gash on his face will take a stitch or two—probably will scar. Various bumps and bruises. It's a miracle, but I don't believe there are internal injuries. He'll be sore, but he should be up and around in a few days. I gave him a shot for the pain."

"That's all?" Tabitha's dawning cry made Abner swallow.

"That's enough, young lady. But all in all, he'll do." The doctor closed his case and glared up at Abner. "Now, sir, do you mind if I go back to the hospital when I've finished here?"

"I'll walk with ya."

"No need. I know this mountain, and you can—uh— call on me anytime. I'm Dr. Carmen, by the way." He held out a hand and Abner wrung it with silent gratitude.

Once the *Englisch* doctor had gone, after a brief consultation with Aenti Fern, Abner turned back to the room to find Tabitha with her face in her hands. Her small shoulders shook as she sobbed.

"*Kind,*" he said roughly, hurt to see her cry. "He will be well. Ya heard the doc."

"I know. I know. It's a relief, that's all."

"*Jah,* but remember, ye've got a lifetime together, *Gott* willing."

She nodded, and he left the room with a last look at the *buwe.*

Anke did what she always did when she was worried— she cooked. The Stolfus kitchen brimmed with a mélange of *gut* smells, cooked to ward off bad news. But she looked up from peeling apples for a strudel when the back door was flung open.

It was Abner, and she waited, searching his face.

"The *buwe* will survive."

She dropped her spoon and raised her apron to her eyes. "Ach, thanks be ta *Gott*."

She rocked from side to side, and then she felt Abner's great arms around her as he made awkward sounds of comfort from the back of his throat.

She let herself lean against him a little and heard the groan that was wrung from him. She would have backed away, but he caught her close, slowly pulling down the apron from her face. She knew that she must look a sight—red, blotchy skin, no doubt, and her nose still damp. But he kissed her. Once. Twice. Again.

"Abner, we cannot. . . ."

"Stop saying that," he rumbled, and she looked up to see a devastating smile on his handsome face.

It would be so easy to give in to his kisses, but her mind screamed in memory. She wrenched herself backward. "I won't!" she cried fiercely. "I tell ya, I won't again."

"Anke?"

She looked up in surprise to see that it was Abner and not her wicked *oncle* who towered over her. "I—I'm sorry," she whispered.

She felt him let her *geh* and she wanted to run from him once more, but his blue eyes spoke of trust and caring and all those things she knew she didn't deserve to have in life because she was dirty. If Abner only knew . . .

She straightened her spine and shook her head at him resolutely. "Ya will jest have ta understand. I cannot ever—have a relationship. Never."

Abner continued to smile down at her. "I am very

strong, Anke. Please, won't you tell me what scares you so?"

"*Nee*, I—"

She broke away from him abruptly when the swinging wooden door between the kitchen and living area was pushed open.

John Stolfus entered and looked at them curiously, then seemed to refocus. "Anke . . . Matt's going to be fine! Let's bake a cake!"

She was only too glad to agree, avoiding Abner's eyes and going to fetch her cake pans.

Matthew opened his eyes and felt as if he'd been on the losing end of a terrific battle. It seemed an effort even to breathe.

"Matthew?" Her voice was honey soft and it enticed him to turn his head, though the effort cost him.

He blinked at her; her beauty was so bright, it seemed like *gut* medicine to his soul. "You're so lovely . . . How is Big Jim?"

"He's fine," she said, then bent and placed a soft kiss on his mouth.

"Mmm. . . . Wish I could do something about that kind of kiss."

"What would you do?" She leaned forward to press her mouth along the arch of his throat, kissing him with burning little sucks of her lips.

"I'd thank you, for saving my life."

She pulled back. "What do you mean?"

"You and that great gray hound. You were there

somehow that day in the forest with the widow-maker. I saw you—in my dream."

She stared down into his eyes. "*Gott* must have revealed this to you."

He smiled. "Maybe. Maybe he wanted me to know how fierce a wife I have."

"And do you like—fierce?" Her voice sounded tentative, and he longed to pull her into his arms.

"*Jah*, I think I lo—"

He broke off in frustration as Aenti Fern admitted Bishop Kore into the room. Tabitha got to her feet and moved aside.

"Ach, Tabitha, my dear *maedel* . . . If I could have a few moments alone with the groom?"

Matthew tried to throw her a don't-leave expression, but she was already slipping into the other room.

He stared up at Bishop Kore and wondered what the *auld* man would say.

"So, my *buwe*. Abner says someone wants you dead. How do ya feel about it?"

Matthew considered the ominous words spoken in light tones. "I'm against it."

"Me too."

Matthew nodded. "*Gut.*"

"How do you feel about groundhogs?"

"*Gut.*"

"All right, then. I'll leave ya with that."

"*Danki.*"

"No trouble at all, *sohn*." Bishop Kore left the room and Tabitha soon returned.

"What did he say?" she asked in confidential tones.

"Death. Life. Groundhogs. Pretty much the usual."

* * *

Tabitha slipped through the woods, ignoring the fine drizzle of rain that pattered on the leaves overhead. She had left Matthew sleeping in Aenti Fern's care. And now she left the trail and continued on another three-quarters of a mile, then skirted around the creek bank and moved to a rocky outcropping, and then a cave that was once a bear's den, now long deserted. She moved aside some brush and entered the cave, reaching automatically for the lantern that was kept high on the right side of the rock.

Turning up the light and holding it aloft, she nearly jumped out of her skin when Christi, Big Jim's *dochder*, stepped out of the gloom.

"What are you doing in here?" Tabitha demanded. "You nearly scared me to death."

"I'm sorry . . ." the young girl said contritely. "I followed you here the other day and just figured you might *kumme* back today. I'm also sorry about your *mann*."

Tabitha slowly regained control of herself. "*Danki*, Christi. And I know you're here about the wood. . . ."

"Yes, ma'am."

"Well . . . *kumme* on back." Tabitha led her young friend deep into the recesses of the cave. She lifted the oilskin tarps that covered her work bench and revealed her tools and her most recent carving, a small eagle poised in midflight.

"Ach, my," Christi murmured in delight. She inched forward and gently put a fingertip to the nearly finished bird. "Your work is beautiful."

"*Danki*. He's still got wing work yet," Tabitha offered. "It's another creature for Abigail's shelf at the pottery."

"Don't folks wonder where she gets 'em?"

Tabitha shrugged. "You know how private she is—probably no one is willing to ask. Anyway, I've told her what I've told you. I make them. I'm glad to own up to that—shunning or *nee*."

Christi shivered a bit in the shadowed light. "I wouldn't like ta be shunned, but it's in me—ta work the wood. I feel it."

"Well, I feel it too," Tabitha said, patting Christi's shoulder. "Now, let me show you what a tiny lathe can do."

Chapter Twenty-Three

Matthew had been up and around for a week when he decided to go back to the mill. He went, of course, while Tabitha was off doing some errand for Anke.

He had *kumme* very close to telling his *frau* that he thought he was in love with her . . . but there had always been some interruption. And now, the more he considered, the surer he was that being in love and loving were two very different things. He wanted to get past the raw emotion and find something that would endure for all time. He thought about the fossil rock that Bishop Kore had given them his first day at Blackberry Falls; it certainly was something that endured. . . .

He broke off in midthought when the mill came into view. Even from a distance, he could tell by some men's postures that he was not the most welcome person at their workplace. But he moved on and felt better when Big Jim called to him, then drew him aside.

"Hey, Matt, *gut* ta see ya up and around."

"*Danki*, but I think Tabitha would have a fit if she knew I was down here."

Jim nodded. "Well, ta tell ya the truth, Matt, there are some fellas who think ya might be bad luck, seeing how you were almost hit by that widow-maker and then the log pile falling . . . ach, and the fire."

Matthew shrugged. "Bad luck? Don't tell me some men believe in that superstitious nonsense?"

"Blackberry Falls is a back hollow, Matt. There's things that *geh* on back here that probably don't happen in yer neck of the woods. Ya gotta understand. Mebbe it would be better if ya took another couple days off."

"Maybe I will, Jim, but first I've got to talk to John."

He shook his friend's hand and made his way past the other men at the mill, coolly meeting the eyes of each who would look at him. He gave a brief knock on the office door, then walked in. John looked up from his desk with a bit of surprise showing on his broad face.

"Hiya, Matt! Didn't know you were coming in today."

"I just thought it would be a good idea to get back into a routine. I could still stack wood with my broken arm."

"That's true. True indeed. But what do you say to us staying in here and looking over the books and the operation for a few days?"

"John, do you believe I'm bad luck?"

"Bad luck? *Nee*, but you make the mill a more dangerous place because someone wants you gone. I can't take that kind of risk around my workers."

"But you do realize that the would-be murderer is one of your own men?"

Matthew watched his *fater*-in-law sigh. "There's another possible explanation for the accidents. I've considered that you might be a bit lacking in cautiousness—never having worked wood before."

Matthew opened his mouth to protest, but then remembered no one here knew about his experience in furniture making. Closing his mouth, he had to agree to work the books with John. But he was determined to find out who it was that wanted him dead, and soon. . . .

Anke had sent Tabitha over to Cubby's to get some mushrooms for the cubed steak supper she wanted to slow cook all day. And after dredging the meat in flour and panfrying it, she added it to the greased pan and cut up a whole onion to place on top. Then she mixed her own brown gravy into the pan and sat down to wait for Tabitha to return.

She sighed aloud in the empty kitchen, not wanting to admit that she missed Abner's company. He hadn't been around much during the past week, and she decided that he must have finally taken her seriously when she'd told him she could never have a relationship with him. At the thought, and much against her will, she found her eyes swimming with tears, which she hastily brushed away. The screen door banged open and she looked up, expecting Tabitha.

But it was Abner, and her heart began to pound in her chest as if she were a *maedel*. All the same, she kept her face calm and composed. "Abner. There's fresh coffee or tea if you'd like."

He grunted and sat down at the well-scrubbed table opposite her. She folded her hands neatly in front of her, not wanting to reveal their faint shaking. But then she saw how work-worn her hands appeared, showing her age in a bad light, and she almost slid them into the folds of her apron. But Abner suddenly reached out with lean-fingered hands and covered hers with his own.

"Anke . . ."

She watched him struggle over what to say, and she waited, irresistibly fascinated.

"Anke, I . . . My cabin needs a woman's touch. I mean—it's not as clean as it might be. Do you think you could . . . would you please . . ."

"Clean it?" she asked flatly.

He appeared deflated. "*Jah*."

She nodded, disappointed for some reason and even more frustrated when he slid his hands away from hers, leaving her feeling *auld* and alone. . . .

But I can't have it both ways, can I? Anke, the house-keeper, who will never marry, or Anke, the woman who wants to believe . . .

When Tabitha entered Cubby's, she avoided the gaze of Sam Fisher and kept her eyes on Grace, who looked as if she was struggling not to cry. Tabitha slipped her basket over her arm and casually made her way to where Grace was straightening up the jam jars on a large shelf. Tabitha noticed that the shelf hid both her and Grace from Sam's view at the back counter. Tabitha was uncertain how to talk to Grace after Anke's point that leaving was "not so easy a thing." But she was determined to give Grace some small sign of support, and when the other woman's hand came down atop a Mason jar of strawberry jam, Tabitha covered her fingers with her own. Grace seemed to appreciate the gesture for a moment, but then quickly pulled away.

"What can I get for ya, Tabby?" Grace asked as some other women shoppers came into the store.

"Fresh mushrooms, if you have them." Tabitha thought how incongruous it was to be speaking of mushrooms when another woman's world stood in shambles, but she accepted the container of white mushrooms and paused to speak to the other women present.

"Hello," Tabitha said, smiling at the two wives whose husbands worked at the mill.

They responded, but Tabitha noted that they kept their eyes averted from her face.

"Is something wrong?" she asked politely.

They both shook their heads, but then Regina, the more outspoken of the two, spoke up. "We can't talk ta ya, Tabby."

"Whyever not?"

Regina leaned close. "Our men think your husband is a hex."

Tabitha's laughter bubbled up. "What? What are you talking about?"

"Bad things have been happening ever since he come here, things at the mill."

"But you know it's not Matthew—they've been accidents." Her laughter faded at the somber looks on the other women's faces. "You're being ridiculous."

But even as she said the words, she felt a vise of anxiety grip her heart. Her community depended on the mill for work and a livelihood. Anything or anyone who threatened the mill could easily awaken the *auld* beliefs that still permeated Blackberry Falls and attracted the community's hatred.

She left the store in a sober mood. Her thoughts ran so deep that she didn't hear Christi calling her until the girl was right next to her.

"Tabitha?"

"What? Ach, *jah*, Christi. . . . How are you?"

"I'm *gut*, but someone stole the eagle that you gave to Abigail."

Tabitha stopped still. "What?"

"*Jah*, I went over there this morning and we noticed it was gone."

"Who would steal it?" Tabitha mused aloud.

Christi shrugged. "Don't know."

Tabitha decided she had bigger fish to fry with people in the community believing Matthew was a hex, so she bade the girl goodbye and walked on.

Abner hurriedly finished scrubbing his kitchen table, then went to work on the cookstove with a vengeance. Anke was due to arrive at any moment—to clean his cabin. *Why can't I say what I want to say around that woman?* he asked himself. *Although half the time I don't know what it is that I want to say.*

He nearly jumped when there was a timid knock on his door. He walked through the cabin, his eyes quickly skimming over the living room to make sure everything was in *gut* shape. Then he opened the front door.

Anke stood there, laden down with a bucket, a mop, and cleaning soap.

"I'm here," she said.

She sounded tired, and he hastened to help take the items she'd brought with her. "*Kumme* in," he invited, trying to keep the mop handle from hitting him in the face.

She brushed past him, and he had to keep an iron hand on himself when he smelled the fresh scent of her—like wind and rain mixed together.

In all the years they'd known each other, she'd very rarely *kumme* to his cabin, and now he felt all thumbs as he dumped her supplies in the corner and turned to gesture awkwardly at the room.

"Ya can see things are quite a mess."

"*Jah*," she said drily. "I can smell the beeswax and lemon oil, Abner. Why did ya ask me ta *kumme*?"

Because I want ta spend time with ya. Touch ya. Love ya. Ask ya if you'd marry me . . .

He took a step backward from his surprising thoughts and put his foot into the metal cleaning bucket with a clanging racket.

He felt foolish, but then Anke started to smile and finally to laugh. The sound was enchanting to him and he stood stock-still, listening.

Then he saw her become sober and begin to retreat into the shell she hid behind so often.

"Don't," he whispered. "Don't hide, Anke."

He was surprised to see her gaze drop and a bitter half smile come to her full lips.

"Ya don't understand, Abner. It's me—inside—who I really am that would shock ya."

"Why not give me that chance?"

"Because I—" She lifted her chin. "Because I care for ya. Now *sei se gut*, I've said all that I can. . . . Please let me be or I'll . . . I'll leave Blackberry Falls and never return."

"Ya don't mean that." He spread his hands helplessly before him.

"*Jah*, I do."

She pushed open the screen door and left him, still standing in the cold bucket.

Tabitha leaned over Matthew in his place beside her bed. He'd insisted, even with his injuries, that he still sleep on the floor. And she'd found, much to her chagrin, that her *mann* could be as stubborn as she.

"I wonder," she said meditatively, flicking her hair back over her shoulder so it wouldn't get in his face. "Are you a hex?"

He smiled up at her. "It's you who has bewitched me, *mei* sweet, not the other way around."

"Hmmm, perhaps. But today I heard two women— wives to mill workers—say that you are indeed a hex."

She watched his smile fade. "Ach, don't tell me any more of this superstitious nonsense. Your *daed* even had me doing the books today instead of working in the mill. The men also fancy me to be bad luck."

"You haven't asked me what I think." She reached down and gently touched his healing cheek.

"And what might that be, *Frau* King?"

She was glad to see that some of his normal *gut* humor

had been restored. "I think—if you are a hex, that you're not a very *gut* one. Because it's only you who keeps getting hurt. And I worry about that." She hadn't meant to sound so serious, but he'd heard her worry; he stretched his unbroken arm and hand upward to run a lean finger down her cheek.

"Don't worry, Tabitha. *Gott* will see me through."

And with that she had to be content.

Chapter Twenty-Four

"I've got bad news. Amy Dienner was murdered," Abner said without preamble the following day. "Big Jim found her body down by the creek."

For a moment silence reined in the Stolfus kitchen, where breakfast had begun.

John Stolfus put down his coffee cup. "How can this be true?"

Abner paced the floor. He didn't have an answer. Never had such a thing happened in Blackberry Falls. "I don't know, John, but Jim found this in her hand." He stopped at the head of the table and put down the small, carved eagle.

Dried bloodstains marred the wood, but the workmanship was that of a master carver. Abner let his eyes drift round the table and his gaze settled on Matthew.

"I've got to tell ya, *buwe*, that some men say that it was you who did this work—and the killin'."

"Me?" Matthew's surprise was obviously genuine.

"You're an outsider still."

"I couldn't carve something like that. . . ."

"But a woman could," Tabitha said softly.

John Stolfus slammed down his hand on the table in an uncharacteristic display of anger, and the eagle fell over. "What are you saying, Tabitha? You must be *narrisch* with worry for Amy—no woman may do woodworking in Blackberry Falls. You know this and you could be shunned for even uttering such a lie!"

"Why?" Matthew spoke up. His very question was a challenge. "Why can no woman carve?"

Abner cleared his throat in the abrupt silence. "John, we'd best *geh* down ta the mill. The bishop and the men have gathered down there. Tabitha—if ya want ta, *geh* with Anke here ta comfort LucyDienner—It's a woman's place."

He looked briefly at Anke, and when he passed her, he squeezed her hand for a second, then went back outside, glad to leave the dangerously charged atmosphere of the kitchen behind.

Tabitha steeled herself as they entered the Dienners' kitchen through the back door. Aenti Fern was there and Lucy Dienner, as well as Grossmuder Mildred and several other women from the community. Tabitha's eyes were drawn irresistibly to the kitchen table, where Amy lay beneath a white sheet that had been drawn up to her bare shoulders. Her eyes were closed and her long red hair curled about her. She looked more peaceful in death than she had in life—despite the way she'd died. Tabitha noted the brutal-looking bruises around Amy's white throat when Aenti Fern moved briskly out of the way.

"Lucy—it's hard fer me ta tell ya, but it's obvious, yer girl died by someone strangling her. I'm sorry."

Lucy looked steadily at Aenti Fern, despite the tears that dampened her cheeks. "I know Amy wasn't the best behaved of *maedels*, but she didn't deserve ta die like this."

Aenti Ruth nodded and continued. "Yer right, Lucy, but I have ta ask—was there any one man she favored?"

Tabitha saw Lucy Dienner shake her head. "*Nee*, not that I know of."

Tabitha wanted to speak up, but she could find no voice to mention the gruff voice of the man she'd heard from the other room when she'd been making pasta salad. She couldn't tell who it had been then and she felt the memory was now even more hazy.

"And look at her right hand," Aenti Fern commented. "It's as if some impression has been made, as if she fought hard with some object and the base has been imprinted into her hand."

"The eagle carving," Tabitha murmured in surprise.

"*Jah*," Aenti Fern agreed, turning to glance at her. "I gave that carving to Abner this morning, to see what he might discover. It was in Abigail's shop and either Amy or her killer must have taken it."

Tabitha nodded. "Perhaps we should *geh* to the police in Farwell."

Aenti Fern shrugged. "*Jah*, but ta what end? They will say that it is our right ta settle this among ourselves, and I would agree. But in any case, the murderer is the man who bears the wounds of this carved eagle on his body. And the murderer is one of our own, of this I'm sure."

"How do ya know?" Amy's *mamm* asked listlessly.

"Amy was not surprised, I think. She faced her attacker and knew him."

Just then, Herr Dienner came in through the back door and wiped his feet overlong on the mat. "Coffin's done," he said, then took out a red hankie and blew his nose. "Bishop Kore says the funeral is set for tomorrow." Tabitha noted that he kept his gaze down, careful not to look at the table. He backed out the door a few seconds later.

And Tabitha was relieved when Anke said they might *geh* home to prepare to host the community after the funeral the next day.

Matthew followed Abner and John on the path that led to the mill. Each step he took seemed to pound a refrain: "Outsider . . . outsider." He ran the fingers of his left hand over the small wooden eagle that he'd scooped up on his way out of the door earlier. He heard Tabitha's words again in his mind: "But a woman could . . . a woman could carve. . . ." For some reason it seemed very important to understand what lay at the heart of this strange rule about carving. He felt in his bones that the mystery had much to do with the loss of Amy Dienner's life—even more than the blood that stained the wood.

He refocused quickly, though, when he saw a group of men barring the entrance to the mill. John stepped forward, clearly angry.

"What is the meaning of this? Why aren't you all at work?"

Big Jim stepped forward and nodded his head deferentially. "We mean *nee* harm, John. Some of the men here feel like it's not safe ta work around Matt. I don't believe this—"

"Ach, stop pussyfootin' around, Jim," one of the men

toward the back called. "We cannot work with a hex or a murderer neither."

With a grim look, Matt shook his head and lifted his broken right arm in its cast. "Murderer? Hardly . . . The poor *maedel* met her end, true, but I could not have done such a crime. Why don't you look to yourselves to find the murderer?"

A low rumble from the group of men sounded ominous in the morning air, but John roared out, and the noise quieted.

"My *sohn*? The murderer of that poor child? I tell you that any one of you who would accuse him accuses me. You can walk off the job right now because I won't have you working here. You can find a job somewhere else!"

The threat was harsh, and meant to be. Surely no man would want to leave the mill—it would most likely mean leaving Blackberry Falls.

But a gruff voice spoke up. "Well, that's fine with us, John Stolfus. Me and Micah are walkin' now."

Asa Zook sauntered forward with a nervous-looking Micah behind him. Clearly, the younger *bruder* had *nee* desire to leave.

"*Geh* on, then!" John growled. "And don't bother coming back."

Matthew didn't move as Asa passed, and it was surely no mistake when Asa brushed close to him with a low growl. Matthew didn't mind the insult; he'd half expected it. But he glanced down at Asa's forearm during the momentary exchange and saw what appeared to be a long scratch. Matthew reached out his good arm and caught Asa, holding him fast.

"How did you get that mark?"

"What's it ta you? I got it in the shop this morning, probably more of yer hexin'." Asa wrenched his arm away, and Matthew fingered the pointed wing of the carved eagle in his pocket. He wondered if he'd just let a murderer walk. Abner moved close and would have held Asa, but Matthew shook his head slightly. It might be better for the community if Asa Zook left Blackberry Falls for *gut*.

Anke glanced over to Tabitha, making sure that the cocoa and confectioner's sugar were being properly mixed with the melted butter. They were on their ninth cake and the kitchen counters were beginning to be full.

"It'll be a sad day tomorrow," she said as Tabitha put down the whisk and then poured the hot icing into a perfect shiny layer atop the cooled sheet cake.

"*Jah*, it was hard—seeing Amy lying there. I thought a lot of strange things and regretted that I'd had words with her not long ago. She was so very young."

"Not much younger than ya be, and I say—until the murderer is caught—that ya let Abner *geh* with ya everywhere."

"But I'm married, Anke. A grown woman . . ."

"Who needs guarding."

"Who needs guarding?"

Anke tensed up when Abner came in through the back door. Matthew followed.

"What did ya say?" Abner went on. "Who needs guarding?"

"Ach, Anke says she fears for my life," Tabitha said. "And I appreciate that concern—"

"As you should," Matthew said. "I don't know what I'd ever do without you."

Anke glanced at Abner and found him staring intently in her direction. The kitchen hummed with the unspoken words in Anke's mind. *I don't know what I'd ever do without you. . . .*

Late that *nacht*, Tabitha lay quietly in bed, staring up at the rough-beamed ceiling of her room. Matthew's words of the morning fluttered through her brain like clean sheets of laundry dancing in the wind. *I don't know what I'd ever do without you. . . .* She'd stared up into his intense green eyes and had seen both truth and surprise mingled there, almost as if he had only just then realized that he believed what he'd said.

"You're very quiet," he murmured, his deep voice drifting up to her from the floor where he lay.

She rolled over and inched her way to the side of the bed, staring down at him in the mellow lantern light. His *gut* arm was bent and rested on his forehead, and she could see the thatch of dark hair at the juncture of his arm and shoulder. She let her gaze trail down his bare chest to where the quilt tangled about his waist.

"I suppose I'm thinking," she offered.

"Ach, me too."

"What about?" They spoke in unison and then laughed together.

"Did you mean what you said in the kitchen?" she asked, hearing the uncertainty in her own voice.

He didn't seem to hesitate, and it pleased her. "About

saying I wouldn't know what to do without you? *Jah*, it's true, *mei frau* . . . it's true."

"*Danki*," she said simply.

"You don't have to thank me for the truth."

"But not everyone values the truth as much as you do."

He seemed to quiet then, and she glanced down once more to find that his eyes were closed and he appeared to be asleep.

Tabitha sighed softly in the stillness of the room, then fell into a dreamless sleep herself.

Chapter Twenty-Five

The next morning was cool and clear and the scent of the mountains filled the souls of those gathered for Amy Dienner's funeral. The women and children stood gathered on one side of the coffin and grave and the men on the other. The coffin had the top third of it cut out and replaced with a pane of glass. It sat on a raised platform so that once Bishop Kore was done preaching, everyone might circle the casket and see Amy's face for the last time.

Those gathered were quiet when the bishop began to speak.

"Many people in our lives help us ta know how ta live," Bishop Kore began. "But very few teach us how ta die."

Matthew tried to wrap his head around the statement but also felt a fresh surge of guilt at the same time. He'd known the previous nacht that he should have told his *frau* the truth about why he'd answered the ad. But everything was so different now. . . . He knew that she'd *kumme* to mean so much to him; his heart expanded as he thought of her. It was a strange thing to fall in love at a funeral, but he did. New life . . . new life following death. It is Gott's way . . . He sought Tabitha's trim form in the group standing on the opposite side of the coffin and saw her holding Christi's hand. She'd make a *gut* mother, he thought tenderly. One who taught by example and led with love . . .

He refocused on Bishop Kore and heard the wisdom in the words of the *auld* man.

"We may think that because Amy died by a violent act that she remains somehow part of that violence, that we will never be able to remember her without thinking of her violent death. But *Derr Herr*, too, died a violent death, one of cruelty and heartlessness. Yet it is His new life that we remember—His triumph over the grave. So shall Amy triumph, and we shall remember her with kindness."

Matthew bowed his head and solemnly began the walk around the coffin. As he glanced down at Amy's pale face, he thought of how fleeting both love and life were, and how equally precious.

Later, at the Stolfus *haus*, Tabitha bent over to serve tea to Grossmuder Mildred, carefully guiding her aged fingers to the handle of the cup.

"*Danki, kind*. I'll take a piece of Anke's pumpkin cake as well."

"I'll *geh* and get it." Tabitha tried to bring as much comfort through gracious hosting as she could to the situation.

She walked back to the kitchen and nearly ran head-long into Elam Smucker, who had on his postal bag. She'd nearly forgotten that it was Tuesday, the day Elam usually walked to Farwell for the mail.

"Excuse me, Tabitha dear. I've got letters for your *fater* and one for your, uh, husband."

"I'll take them," she offered, intent on reaching the cakes in the kitchen. It only registered vaguely to her that this would be the first letter that Matthew had received from Renova since their wedding.

She absently slid the envelopes into the pocket of her apron and sidestepped Elam when he wouldn't move. "Tabitha," he said low as she brushed past. "I know you cannot be happy with that—outsider. Let's forget this sham of a marriage you have made and run away together somewhere. . . ."

She glanced at him with a surprised but derisive smile. "Your mother would be in attendance, Elam. Whatever privacy would we have then?" She resisted the urge to step on one of his flat feet and entered the kitchen.

Matthew was having a drink of water at the table and Anke didn't seem to be around. Matthew looked up as she entered.

"What's the matter?" he asked as she felt him search her face.

"Elam Smucker. That reminds me, here's a letter for you from Renova," she said briefly.

"Ah . . . well—" He placed the letter on the table. "Let me put any such nonsense as Elam Smucker presents out of your mind." He stood and rounded the corner of the table to take her in his arms.

Tabitha smiled up into his handsome face. "Anyone could *kumme* in here."

"Mmm-hmm. And all they would see is a man kissing his wife." He punctuated his words with kisses that led from behind her right ear to her neck. She shivered in response and reached to loop her arms around his neck. She arched her back, pressing herself full against him and returned his kisses boldly.

He groaned as their lips met in wet heat, and the sound drove her further. She pulled the back of his chestnut hair, then twined it around her fingers.

"Ummm . . . Tabitha. I—I think—"

"So do I," she breathed.

He smiled against her mouth. "Tonight."

"*Jah*," she whispered.

"Ahem!"

They broke apart as her fater entered through the back door of the kitchen. "Don't mind me! I'm glad to see you *bussing*. It'll be time for *grandkinner* soon."

Tabitha felt her face flush, but looking up at Matthew, she saw him composed and smiling. *Tonight . . . Jah, tonight . . .*

Anke wearily backed up from the narrow canning pantry with some extra dish towels in her hands and ran directly into Abner. She knew it was he by the strength and height of his body and by the low rumble of pleasure that reverberated through his chest.

"Abner," she whispered. "Let me *geh*."

She turned in his arms and stared up at him to find him looking concerned. "No one can see us here, and besides, I'm worried that all of this preparation and serving is too much for ya."

She huffed and slapped the dish towels against his arm. "I am *nee* so *auld*, Abner Mast."

"I didn't say that, but ya look tired."

"I'm not that either—though mebbe a little." The admission seemed to make her wearier, and part of her longed to sag against him.

He must have sensed her feelings because he moved closer and pressed her to him. She breathed in the fresh-mint scent of him and felt herself relax for the first time that day. It was an odd sensation, to lean against another, to take refuge and comfort from the cares of the day. But she would not indulge her senses for long and soon pushed against his broad chest.

"I've got ta take these towels back. There's dishes ta wash."

"Fine. Then I'll be washin' them."

"You're *narrisch*."

"Mebbe. Mebbe not. But I'm washin' those dishes."

She brushed past him and sighed. *If he was willin' ta help, why not let him. . . .*

Abner rolled up his shirtsleeves and turned to face the kitchen sink. He ignored the clucks of disapproval that Anke was making somewhere behind him and plunged a small stack of plates into the sudsy water.

He started to whistle and let his mind drift to a place where he might gladly do homey chores for Anke if she were his *frau*. . . . His hands slowed in the warm water. My *frau* . . . He tasted the thought like warm, sticky toffee against his tongue. It was sweet and so within his grasp, if only Anke would tell him what bothered her so much. He knew from her response at Blackberry Falls that she had enjoyed kissing him, but he also knew that there was so much more to love—something he'd experienced little of in his own life—perhaps Anke was the same. . . .

Later that *nacht*, Matthew eased down his suspenders and slid off his shirt. Although it was still high summer, the night air coming through the screened windows was chilly, and he crouched at the fireplace in Tabitha's room to build a small fire. He wanted the warm intimacy the flames brought to the shadows of the room because he fully intended to make love to his wife that *nacht*.

He looked up when the bedroom door opened and Tabitha entered, looking flushed and beautiful. "The fire is nice," she commented.

"You are nice," he returned.

She started to cross the room but then stopped and bent over to pick up something from the floor. . . .

Chapter Twenty-Six

She picked up the piece of paper from the floor and turned it over, automatically scanning the first lines.

Dear Big Bruder,

How are things going? How is the incidental wife and the internship? Have you inherited Stolfus Lumber and Woodworking yet? I've got to say that things are a bit boring around here since you've been gone, but it must be working out since you haven't come running home to your beloved tools.

Write soon,
Caleb

Tabitha felt her knees give way and she sank to the floor. She read the brief letter in full, then lifted her head to stare at Matthew.

He had risen to his feet, and there was a stricken look on his face. "Tabitha—don't—"

"Don't what?" she whispered. "You answered my ad—

you decided to come here, knowing full well what Stolfus Lumber was. . . ."

"I did know, that's true, but I didn't want to inherit anything. I never thought about it—never. I wanted an internship, and your offer seemed like a good way to get one."

"And an incidental wife," she choked. "Did you want that as well?"

"I didn't know you then, but I've *kumme* to love and care for you."

"Liar!" She got to her feet and flung the word at him, longing to hurt him with the reality of what he'd done.

"I am that," he admitted, but it did little to bring her satisfaction. "But I haven't lied about how I feel for you. I should have told you the truth from the beginning, yet it never seemed to be the right time—"

"*Jah*," she said bitterly. "The truth is inconvenient that way."

"Tabitha, I've *kumme* to love everyone here at Blackberry Falls. I know now that what I did was wrong. I know you're hurt. I want to make things right. Let's please talk—"

"I want you gone," she said, her voice quavering. "Out of this *haus*; away from Blackberry Falls. *Geh* back to your home and wait for another ad that you can use to bring pain to people who open their lives to you."

"I want to—"

"I don't care what you want," she replied in savage tones. "My *fater* called you his *sohn*. I called you *mei* husband and many others called you friend. You've lied to everyone, and I mean what I say. Leave. Tonight."

She swallowed hard and turned her back on him,

waiting until she heard him gather his shirt and open and then close the door behind him. . . .

Matthew slid on his shirt over his cast and walked down the steps of the Stolfus haus. His heart felt like lead in his chest and tears pricked the backs of his eyes. Everything Tabitha had accused him of was true. . . . *I should not have answered that ad . . . but what would my life be if I'd never met Tabitha or* kumme *to Blackberry Falls . . . ?*

He was making his way to the front door when he heard Abner call his name. Matthew turned slowly and stayed in the shadows, away from where Abner sat framed by the firelight.

"Where are ya off ta, *buwe*?"

"I'm leaving, Abner." There. The truth, once said, seemed so easy. *Why did I think it was hard?*

"Leaving? What are ya talkin' about?"

"I'm a liar, Abner, and a thief. I answered Tabitha's ad, knowing full well about Stolfus Lumber and Woodworking. I wanted an apprenticeship. . . . I thought of having to marry as just a minor side problem, and I stole love and affection from Tabitha, John—everybody."

Matthew waited, expecting anything from cold dismissal to outright rage, but he was not prepared for soft words.

"A liar, you say? Then I'd have to say that there are other lies that have been carried on and guarded well in this *haus*—some for years." Abner's tone was meditative.

"What—what do you mean?"

"Have you happened to see among Tabitha's possessions a carved wooden ladle?"

Matthew's mind flashed back to the moments before Amy Dienner had entered Tabitha's bedroom, when he'd found the beautiful ladle in the bottom drawer. "*Jah*. I wondered who made it for Tabitha."

"*Jah*, ya might wonder that."

"Abner . . . you sound cryptic and *mei frau* just threw me out for being a liar—I don't have much time left to try to decipher what you're saying."

"It was Tabitha's mother's wish that the ladle be given ta the *boppli* as a gift."

"Okay . . . so Tabitha told me her *mamm* passed away after nursing Bishop Kore's wife."

"That's what Miriam wanted Tabitha ta believe."

Matthew stepped closer to the firelight. "Wait. What?"

"Miriam Stolfus was as fine a wood carver as anyone I've ever seen—even, perhaps, to the point of surpassing what her husband could produce."

"A wood carver—a woman wood carver. All right, can you tell me the rest?"

"*Nee*," Abner said flatly.

"Great."

"The rest is for ya ta work out yerself, *buwe*. Ta work out with Tabitha."

"Abner, she won't have anything to do with me. She'll annul the marriage."

"Fight for her, *buwe*. 'Fight the *gut* fight . . .' She will believe in you if she recognizes truth in you."

Matthew shook his head. "I'm not sure I see it in myself."

"Then search for it . . . In the meantime, ya can bunk over at my cabin."

"*Danki*, Abner. I'll try as you say."

* * *

Abner sat at the Stolfus hearth for a bit longer and prayed for Tabitha and the buwe. Then he felt led in his heart to *geh* up the stairs and knock softly on Tabitha's door. It was a long time before she answered, and when the *maedel* did open the door, Abner was met with a stormy face and wildly tousled honey-blond hair.

"What is it, Abner?" she bit out, and he steeled himself against her obvious pain. One part of him felt like wringing the *buwe*'s neck himself, while another considered the advice he'd given by firelight. He sighed aloud as reason won out.

"I know you've been hurt, *kind*."

"Do you?" she asked in bitter tones. "Has the liar won you over as well? I would have thought you made of stronger stuff."

"*Jah*, perhaps, but were ya entirely honest in that ad of yours?"

She glared up at him. "What do you mean?"

"Ya wanted an *Amisch* mail-order groom as an idea mebbe, but did ya want a living, breathing man who makes mistakes but loves ya just the same?"

"You don't know what you're talking about. He lied to me, to you, to everybody."

"There is nothing that cannot be confessed before *Derr Herr*, that cannot be forgiven. Do ya then pretend ta have a higher set of principles than *Gott*?" He waited, half surprised at his own boldness, watching a sea of emotion storm across her beautiful face.

"I'm tired," she whispered finally. "I—I'll think on what you've said."

Abner eased back from the door as she closed it and nodded to himself in the shadows of the hall. *Gott* was on the move this *nacht*. . . .

Chapter Twenty-Seven

Anke was up extra early the next morning to make a raisin bread pudding for breakfast. She had just added the vanilla when she heard a brisk knock at the door that made her jump. She glanced at the windup clock on the counter. Five a.m. She cautiously went to open the door, with the thought running through her head that Amy Dienner's killer had yet to be found. But it was Bishop Kore, looking ruffled and serious.

"Anke, is John up yet?"

"*Nee*. What be the trouble?"

"Well, I hate ta tell ya, but Lydia Smucker passed away in her sleep last *nacht*."

"Elam's *mamm*? But Lydia always seemed as fit as can be."

"I know, but Elam said he went to wake her for their normal tea and she was gone."

"I'll *geh* and wake John. I can't believe we're ta have a second funeral in as many days."

"Close as salmon on a riverbed, but Anke, I want you to know that no one expects you to host the community afterward. You've done enough in the last days. Elam himself says that he will do the hosting after the service."

"Then I'll help with the cooking, same as most folks will."

"All right. Fair enough. *Danki*, Anke."

She wished him a better morning and was about to ease the door closed when Abner's big frame appeared in the dawn shadows.

"I heard," he said briefly.

She nodded and let him in, unprepared for the kiss he gave her on her cheek. She felt young and innocent for a moment and reveled in the emotion.

Matthew lay staring at the wooden beams of Abner's ceiling as dawn crept in through the window as blushing light. *Fight* . . . Abner had said. *Fight for Tabitha*. Something stirred at the back of his mind as he watched the light play over the wood above him. It was one thing that he and Tabitha did not have—their own cabin. *I should have thought of it so much sooner. . . . We can build together—both our lives and our home. If she'll agree . . .*

Tabitha awoke after a fitful *nacht*'s sleep. Her mind and heart had burned within her and she could not forget the stricken look on Matthew's face when he'd tried to apologize; nor could she erase the challenge of Abner's words.

"But I've been hurt so badly, *Gott* . . . " she prayed softly aloud. "He played me for a fool—a joke between him and his *bruder*." She bowed her head and realized that it was truly her pride that had been hurt. And she realized that her pride had never stung so before. She knew that being prideful was never good, especially when it led to a lack of forgiveness. But she also knew that she wanted no resentment on her part toward Matthew. She finally yielded her spirit, allowing *Gott* to have His way in the relationship, and an idea came to her. . . .

Abner sighed as he walked back to his cabin in the dawn of the day. His gentle kiss on Anke's cheek had seemed to free her for a moment from all her sadness, and she had turned her mouth to meet his. Hot blood had surged through his body and he'd stood, enthralled by her soft lips. His senses were filled with her—part the smell of vanilla, part morning's sweet dew, and all wonderful woman. Everything seemed possible to him in the moments she was in his arms. He felt young and free and as connected with a person as he'd ever been before in his life.

"Anke, *sei se gut*, will you be—" He broke off when he heard Tabitha calling Anke's name and muttered beneath his breath. *What was I going to say? Will you be . . . Will you be . . . and he admitted, at some soul level, that he had very nearly asked Anke to be his wife.*

Tabitha pushed the kitchen door open and found Anke standing in the middle of the room with a hand pressed to her lips.

"Anke, what's wrong? Did you see a mouse? Are you

trying not to scream?" Tabitha stared at the older woman in bemusement.

"*Nee*," Anke finally responded, lowering her hand. "I—I was thinking. That's all."

Tabitha came forward and gave Anke a quick hug. "You sound like you're trying to convince yourself. Are you sure that nothing's wrong?"

"Lydia Smucker passed away in her sleep some time during the *nacht*."

"What?" Tabitha exclaimed.

"*Jah*. The bishop stopped by . . . I was just going to wake your *fater*."

"I'll wake him." Tabitha snatched an apple from the wooden bowl on the table and left the kitchen.

Her *fater*'s rooms were on the first floor of the cabin and Tabitha had always enjoyed waking him when she was a *maedel*. But she realized that she had stopped the daily ritual when her da had begun to plague her about marrying. She perceived, as she stood with a gentle hand on the door, that she had truly been angry with her *fater* for insisting she marry. And, once again, Abner's words about the ad and her own motives came back to her.

She knocked a bit louder, and her *daed* called for her to come inside.

Her *fater* was dressed and pulling on his socks when she entered. He looked pleased to see her and she went to sit on the bed by his side.

"You're up early, Tabby. How's Matt?"

"Fine . . . " She carefully slid the uneaten apple into her apron pocket. Whatever she had to work out with her husband, she was not about to trouble her *fater* with the details. "He's fine, but Anke told me that Lydia Smucker passed away last *nacht*."

"Ach, *nee* . . . Elam will be heartbroken."

Tabitha nodded, not caring to dwell on the arrogant Elam. She leaned over and kissed her *daed*'s weather-beaten cheek.

"What was that for?" he asked gruffly.

She smiled. "Because I love you."

Matthew sat on the edge of Abner's kitchen table and worked at securing the pins in his blue shirt. Abner had gone out and Matthew looked up in surprise at the sound of the cabin door opening. Tabitha stood there, framed by the morning's light and looking achingly beautiful, but he watched her with a wary eye. After last *nacht* he felt he could expect and deserved a piece of crockery thrown at his head. But she simply stood with her back to the door, watching him.

"So, Caleb is your younger *bruder*?"

"*Jah*," he replied cautiously, pricking himself with a pin.

"You'll get blood on your shirt. Here, let me." She came forward and he lowered his hands to grip the underside of the table. "Who else is in your family?"

"My *fater*, Caleb, and my *aulder* bruder, Luke. Ach, and my Aenti Joy."

She slid out the top pin of his shirt and then the next. He felt as if he was holding his breath, waiting to see what sweet torture she had devised for him. Another pin was removed, and he drew a shaky breath. "Are you starting from the beginning?" he asked, trying to force his voice to be casual.

"From the beginning." she nodded. "*Jah*, we are."

He nodded in return as she bent forward to lightly kiss his collarbone; he closed his eyes. He felt her splay her fingers across the center of his bare chest, easing his shirt off his shoulders.

"Mmm. . . . Tabitha." He opened his eyes slowly, wanting to prolong the sensation of anticipation—that feeling somewhere between his senses overloading and straightforward lust for his wife. He gripped the table edge tighter and bent forward to kiss her, but she dipped away, latching on to his right shoulder with bold, nipping kisses.

"You're going to leave marks," he observed hoarsely.

"Mmm-hmm," she agreed. "Marks that only you and I shall know about."

"Right . . . Can I return the favor?" He was startled by her abrupt straightening. It was if she had snapped out of some spell. She reached into her apron pocket. "*Nee. Nee* return favors, but I will give you this . . . to bite on."

He took the apple mindlessly, bemused and aroused.

"As I said, we'll start over, Matthew King." Her voice was brisk. "Today."

He watched her spin and walk to the cabin's door; then he bit the apple. . . .

Chapter Twenty-Eight

Tabitha stared down at the plate of ham and scalloped potatoes that she held in her hand. She knew it was one of Anke's specialties, but she'd suddenly lost her appetite when Elam approached her at the gathering after his *mamm*'s funeral.

"Ah, Tabitha. How are you feeling?"

She thought idly that it was an odd question but answered anyway. "I'm fine, but I suppose that I should be asking after you—I'm very sorry about your *mamm*."

"Don't be. She's no doubt in a happier place, after all." He gave her a flat-lipped smile and she glanced around to see if she could find Matthew in the crowd. She saw him, head and shoulders above the group he was talking with, and longed for him to rescue her from this conversation with Elam.

"I might ask how your marriage is going—no doubt you've heard that some have suspected your—uh—*mann* to be the murderer of Amy Dienner."

Tabitha stared at him in amazement. "Are you *narrisch*, Elam, to speak so of my husband, and at your *mamm*'s funeral? Don't talk to me again." She pushed past him, ignoring the stares she received for her abruptness, and made her way to Matthew's side, abandoning her plate. "Let's *geh*," she whispered, standing on tiptoe to reach his ear.

He smiled and nodded, then bid Oncle Nutter a *gut* day. Tabitha was grateful for his hand at the small of her back as they made their way to the front door of Elam's cabin. She drew a deep, refreshing breath once they'd stepped outside.

"What's the matter?"

"Nothing—only Elam Smucker."

"He's quite a snot, I think."

She laughed, her humor restored. "*Jah*, he is at that."

"If he bothers you again, I could have a word with him."

She shook her head. "*Nee*, let's forget him and *geh* to the falls. It's hot enough to wade a bit."

"I'd like to do more than wade."

She looked up to see him looking serious and decided that he meant something more than kissing. "What else would that be?"

"I'd like to talk about the future. I think we should have our own cabin and that you should help me to build it."

"But women cannot—"

"I know," he soothed. "But, if I'm not wrong, you can work with wood and I believe you could teach me much."

She stopped stock-still and stared up at him, her heart pounding with sudden happiness. "You—would let me teach you?"

He bent his head to kiss her tenderly. "*Jah* . . . I'd let you teach me with pleasure."

She felt tears sting her eyes. "How did you know—about me, I mean?"

"I think I sensed on many occasions—and Gott gave me insight—that you seem to come alive when you're with wood."

She laughed in sudden abandon. "And maybe when I'm with you too!"

Abner eased a finger around his shirt collar and thought how stuffy Elam Smucker's cabin was. He'd seen Tabitha and the *buwe* leave a while earlier and wondered if he might get Anke to do the same.

He was tired—both mentally and physically. He felt like the push-pull relationship he had with Anke was sapping his strength. Sometime or another, he'd blurt out the truth to her, as he'd nearly done the other *nacht. I want ta marry her . . . marry. . . .* He had to drag his thoughts back to the moment when he'd seen Anke moving among the guests with a tray of something in her arms.

Anger surged through him. . . . *She is always serving . . . but who serves her?* The question provoked him, and he made his excuses to people as he moved through the crowd to get to Anke. But Bishop Kore suddenly impeded his progress and Abner stifled a groan.

"Abner—bad day today, right? But Anke just gave me this!" The bishop waved a small plate with a piece of chocolate cake on it in front of him. "Know what it's missing?"

"*Jah* . . . peanut butter icing?" Abner wanted to be free, but he could not be rude to the bishop despite his irritation.

"Ach . . . *jah* . . . you've got it. . . . But do you? I mean truly? Do you have the cake, Abner?"

"I plan on it—if I can reach Anke, sir. . . ."

"Ach, Abner . . . ya have a *gut* sense of humor, though

ye'd hide that from the world, I think. . . . Don't fear, I won't tell anyone."

"*Gut . . . Danki*, Bishop." Abner saw Anke move away to the kitchen and stifled the urge to pull the bishop's long beard. He sneezed instead, covering his mouth and pulling out a red hankie from his back pocket. "Ye'll have ta excuse me, sir. . . ."

"Ach, *jah* . . . go on, go on, but remember that the cake without the icing isn't worth having."

"*Jah* . . . I . . . understand."

"*Nee*, ya don't, but *geh*, just the same."

Abner sighed, wiping his nose, and headed for the kitchen area.

Matthew loved the happiness his suggestion of wood-working had brought to his *frau*. She held his hand tightly and smiled up at him as they walked through the forest to Blackberry Falls. He had every intention of trying to kiss her behind the falls, but as they came out of the woods, they both stopped as a majestic buck slowly lifted its head from drinking the fresh water to turn and stare at them.

"He's beautiful," Tabitha whispered.

The deer seemed to decide that he'd presented enough of a show and bounded off through the water and into the forest on the other side.

"I love it when something secret and special is re-vealed to us. . . . I haven't seen a buck that big in a long time," she said.

"And I haven't seen anyone as beautiful as you—ever." He watched the flush *kumme* to her cheeks and reached down to gently cup her fragile jaw in his callused hand. "I want to be marrying you, Tabitha. Marrying for a very long time—like the bishop talked about, remember?"

"*Jah*." He watched her draw a deep breath. "I want that too. I think we have to *geh* about it slowly—feel our way to knowing and understanding each other. And—I think that making love isn't the only important thing we have to focus on—like you said."

He watched her lift her chin, though he sensed that she was embarrassed by her own words and admired her strength of purpose.

"I agree," he said, wondering when he'd said those words. He thought rather ruefully that his earlier delay in completing their vows was probably what she was talking about. He decided at that moment that some cold water was just what he needed. Grabbing her hand, he led her to the streambank.

He had one of her small, well-formed feet in his hands when someone stepped out from behind the falls. He was surprised to see Aenti Fern make her way across the slippery rocks with a small basket over her arm.

"Water's nice. I was washing my smalls—underwear, if ya must know. Now I've got ta git on home."

"Have a nice evening," Tabitha called.

When the *auld* healer was out of earshot, Matthew lay down on the mossy bank and pulled his wife near him. He watched her blue, blue eyes focus on one of his hands and felt the by-now-familiar pain of wanting but not being satisfied. He pressed his lower body against the hard earth and watched Tabitha explore the contours of his hand with her own slender fingers. Her touch was intoxicating, but then she looked up at him with a smile.

"I wonder if the faeries sing when Aenti Fern washes her underwear?" she asked.

He bent and kissed her nose with a grin. "I'd rather imagine that buck wearing a corset, frankly!"

Anke wearily worked the outdoor pump of the Smuckers' well, fetching more water for another pitcher of lemonade. She nearly jumped in surprise when big hands pushed her gently aside and she glanced up into the glare of the sun to stare at Abner's face. His lips were set in a firm line and she thought he seemed angry.

"Anke, tell me, *sei se gut*, when was the last time somebody brought you a glass of something ta drink?"

"What? What do ya say? I have no time fer riddles, Abner Mast. Go on in and let me be."

Abner stopped the pump and took her by her shoulders in a gentle grip. "Anke, as sure as the sun shines tomorrow as *Gott* wills, I am going ta kiss ya here and now if ya don't leave that pitcher fer someone else ta fill."

"Someone younger, mebbe?" she asked, her pride hurt.

"Someone who has not been up since before daybreak," he countered, sliding the glass pitcher carefully from her hand.

She would have said something if he hadn't coughed then, carefully turning away from her.

"Abner, be ya sick?" She stretched up a hand to his forehead as he moved back to face her.

"I'm *nee* sick."

Anke put her hands on her hips. "Then why are ya burning with fever?"

He frowned down at her. "I am not and I don't need to be nursed neither."

"Ach, it's one thing fer ya ta tell me what ta do, but the shoe doesn't fit on the other foot, does it?"

"I've had plenty of fevers alone. Before . . ." His voice trailed off, and Anke felt unbidden tears sting the backs of her eyes.

"Before what, Abner? Before ya got these crazy ideas about me?"

"They're not *narrisch*. . . . I really care . . ."

She watched as he broke off and coughed again, waving the water pitcher.

"That's it, Abner. Home. Ta bed. With me." She felt her face flame at the boldness of her words but saw with relief that he put down the pitcher and started toward the path that led to his cabin. . . .

Chapter Twenty-Nine

"Now there'll be *nee* stroking of the fevered brow and spoonin' me soup," Abner said as he opened the door to his cabin.

"Are ya used ta the *maedels* doin' that fer ya, Abner?" Anke asked drily.

"*Nee*, but I read some such stuff in a book once and it seemed like an awful thing ta hold a man down."

"Ya needn't worry . . . I'm not the stuff books are made of. . . . Just undo yer shirt and git into bed."

He noticed that she sounded flustered and turned his back to lower his suspenders and unpin his blue shirt. He stepped out of his boots and then slid into the big bed, feeling vaguely surprised that he was glad to lie down. He stared across the room at Anke, who was now facing him.

"Close yer eyes and *geh* ta sleep. I'll just sit here a spell," she ordered, moving to a bentwood rocker.

He shook his head slowly. "Rather look at you."

"Well, don't," she said; then she half smiled. "Ya close yer eyes and I'll tell ya a story."

"That sounds *gut*. Never had anyone do that fer me."

"Well, ya should have," she pronounced with a quiet

assurance that seemed to reach back and stir his lonely boyhood heart.

"I'll start the way my *mamm* told it ta me," she began, and he closed his eyes on the soft cadence of her voice. "Once, when the world was a lot smaller, and time moved a lot slower, a little *maedel kumme* ta these very woods ta live with her *Amisch* family. Her folks had died from fever, leaving eight-year-old Priscilla alone but fer her three *aentis*, who'd never approved of their youngest sister running away ta marry an *Amisch* man. Under their guidance, Priscilla grew ta be a fine young woman.

"She loved the ways of the woods and had *nee* fear of the creatures that lived there. She spent many an hour talkin' ta the chipmunks and raccoons and possums, and wandered far afield in her daily rambles. One day, toward the gloaming, when she knew she should be gettin' back ta her *haus*, she came upon a big, wounded bear. She showed *nee* fear but quietly walked up ta the bear's shaggy side and looked at the massive paw that was torn by a large thorn. Then she used both her hands and pulled the painful thorn free. And she took part of her skirt ta wrap up his wound. Then, as it began ta snow, she invited the bear home with her, ta spend the *nacht* by the fire. And the bear followed her home. But her three *aentis* were filled with fear at the sight of the big bear and locked themselves in a cold back bedroom. Still, Priscilla thought they wuz silly and lay down next ta the bear by the hearth's blaze."

"Is he gonna eat her?" Abner heard himself slur with a smile.

"*Nee*, it's a faerie tale."

Something in her tone roused him enough to ask, "Do ya believe in faerie tales, sweet Anke?"

He heard her draw a deep breath, and she took so long to answer, he thought perhaps she'd fallen asleep. "Anke?"

"I think that's enough storytellin' fer yer fever, and I'm not sweet."

He chuckled, then choked back a cough. "Sweet as spun sugar, ya be."

"Uh-huh. I'm gonna fetch ya some tea fer that fever and ask Aenti Fern ta stop by."

"Don't leave," he pleaded, unwilling to lose the unique pleasure of her company alone in his cabin, even if he did feel worse than a swamp rat.

"I'll be back."

"Promise?"

"*Jah*, Abner. I promise ya."

"I want ta hear how the *maedel* makes out with the bear."

He fancied he felt a brush of her lips across his hot forehead and he drank in her warmth, falling deeply asleep.

Matthew bent over the desk, which was illuminated by the lanterns in the bedroom, as he listened to Tabitha's ideas for their cabin and drew rough sketches. He was amazed at her understanding of building and architecture, which included practical ideas like a laundry chute that ran from the second floor down to the first-floor washroom.

"It's a great idea," he said, looking up at her as she leaned over his shoulder. Her pumpkin-colored dress did much to show off the beauty of her eyes and he put down the pencil and turned around on the stool where he sat.

He took both of her hands in his and smiled up at her. "You're a rare creature, Tabitha King. Rare in face, mind, and heart. And as *Gott* wills, we will build this cabin and a life together."

"When can we start? I know my *fater* will provide all the materials, and all the community will help, like a barn raising. . . . That is, if we want them to."

"I would, Tabitha, honestly, but when will you be able to use your skills as a woodworker?"

She bent and placed a saucy kiss full on his mouth. "I'll work at *nacht*; no one will see. I'd like to do the spindles, and lattice, and windowsills. Ach, all the finishing work, and I can easily do that by lantern light."

"Not alone, you're not. Amy Dienner's murderer has yet to be found. I'll *geh* with you to work. But I would like it much better if you could simply be a carpenter in the light of day—with *nee* risk of shunning."

He watched her shrug her slender shoulders. "I don't mind taking the risk. And we can build far enough away that no one will see the light, but I do have one question: When exactly will you sleep if you're working all day and guarding me at *nacht*?"

He laughed. "I still am unsure what the men at the mill think of me working with them, and besides, I'm sure you can find some interesting ways to keep me awake."

She leaned closer to him. "*Jah*, I can."

"Pneumonia?" Anke exclaimed, feeling suddenly sick to her stomach with worry. "Be ya sure?"

She saw Aenti Fern's wry look. "Ya can hear him struggling ta breathe."

Anke cast her eyes over Abner's wide, bare chest and wished she might breathe for him.

"Love him, do ya?"

Anke was both startled and terrified by the question. "*Nee* . . . just I—"

"Mmm-hmm," Aenti Fern replied. "Well, I've got some tea here for ya ta brew for him, and he needs ta throw up that congestion in his lungs. Give him a few drops of ipecac every half hour or so. He'll *kumme* out right."

"Ach, but mebbe ya had better stay. I don't—"

"Anke, ya be many things, but a coward ain't one of them. And the *gut Gott* knows that love is more fearful than hate sometimes."

Anke watched her close her satchel and accepted the tea leaves to brew. She had no reply to Aenti Fern's words, but she knew them to be true. She settled in for a long *nacht*. . . .

Tabitha crept from her bed long after they'd extinguished the lanterns. Matthew still slept on the floor and she moved softly, listening to the sound of his even breathing, until she'd made it to the dresser that housed her shifts. She rooted in the bottom drawer until she'd found the carved wooden ladle and held it carefully in her hands in the moonlight. For some reason it felt very important that she touch it before she embarked on the journey of building a home with Matthew—before carving the wood. . . .

* * *

Abner was dreaming. He felt hot, as though the weight of a bear's heavy fur enveloped him. He felt himself move, lumbering after the beautiful woman who beckoned to him. She brought him inside her cabin and eased him down on the hearth rug. He felt oddly safe and complete. He dozed in the light of the fire and she lay at his back, spooning against him, one arm around his waist.

He heard his own breathing; it seemed hoarse and labored. But still, he slept until a pressing pain in his stomach caused him to sit bolt upright and promptly throw up.

Chapter Thirty

"I don't like bein' fussed over!"

"I know," Tabitha soothed as Abner dodged the spoon she was holding.

"Where's Anke anyway?"

Tabitha hated to lie to him, but she'd given her word.

"Just resting for a bit. I know it'll please her if you would take this medicine, though."

She watched Abner exhale, then swallow the spoonful of herbal tea. "Blah. I'm sick of that stuff and being treated like a *boppli*. I need to get up and stretch my bones. It'll do me *gut*!"

"I suppose a bit of a walk around the cabin would do no harm," Tabitha said as she put down the spoon.

"Ha! I'll walk down to the mill," he roared.

"Hey, what's all the fuss in here?" Matthew asked as he entered the cabin. "Abner, hasn't Tabitha told you about Anke? I would have thought that you—"

"What about Anke?"

Tabitha threw a wry glance at her husband and spoke softly. "She didn't want us to worry you."

"What is wrong with Anke?"

Tabitha had never seen her guardian so upset. "She's sick. Aenti Fern thinks she got it—"

"From nursing me, *nee* doubt."

"Maybe, but she's really doing much better."

Tabitha watched helplessly as Abner pulled on his shirt and boots.

"She's in her room at John's?" he practically growled. *"Jah. . . ."*

"Gut! I'll be goin' over now."

Tabitha listened as the door slammed behind him, then looked at Matthew. "He's acting like he still has a fever," she said.

She saw Matthew's slow smile. "I think he does have a fever—in his blood—and for Anke."

"Anke? What are you talking about?"

"I think Abner wants to be more than friends with Anke."

"I never even noticed," Tabitha mused.

Matthew came forward and caught her in his arms. "Perhaps you've had other things on your mind, sweet."

She stretched up to kiss him. "Perhaps you're right."

Abner took the steps three at a time to get to the second floor of the Stolfus *haus*. He knew that Anke's room was a few doors down from Tabitha's, but he wasn't exactly sure of which door. He listened for female voices, then strode quickly down the hall and knocked.

"Anke!"

Footsteps echoed on the hardwood floor from the other side. Abner hastily ran a hand through his hair as the door was flung open.

He stared down at Aenti Fern's wrinkled and perturbed face.

"Where's Anke?"

"In bed, where ya should be also."

"I want ta see her," he demanded despite Aenti Fern's eye roll in response.

"I'll ask if she wants ta see ya. Wait here."

Abner stared at the wood as the door was shut briskly in his face. He chafed at the delay, but then Aenti Fern reopened the door.

"She doesn't want ta see ya, Abner. *Geh* back ta bed."

She got the door half shut before he automatically shot out an arm and halted the closure. "Fern, I've got ta make sure she's all right."

"She's on the mend, Abner Mast, and she don't need ya ta rile her up."

"Please . . ." He choked out the word and lifted his head when he heard Anke's voice.

"Let him in. . . . It's all right."

Aenti Fern glared up at him. "Five minutes. That's it."

He nodded and slowly stepped into the room as Aenti Fern stepped out. He was unprepared for how wan and sick Anke looked. He went forward and dropped to his knees at her bedside, gently taking her hand in his.

"How are ya?" he asked softly, surprised to feel tears sting his eyes.

"Better now. How are ya?"

He shook his head. "Ya be sick because ya took care of me. I remember ya prayin' over me. I'm so sorry, Anke."

"Ya don't have power over sickness, Abner. Only *Gott* does, and I'll be well again and up and around soon, thanks to *Derr Herr*."

"You're wise, Anke. Too *gut* for the likes of me, if truth be told."

He watched her draw a deep breath. "But there's a lotta truth I guess we don't tell. Not to each other anyways."

"Ya can tell me anything, sweet Anke. Please, won't ya trust me?"

"I—"

Abner frowned as the door opened and Aenti Fern came in. "Time's up. Abner, git up off the floor. She's made it through, praise *Gott*, and yer prayers now might be better spent on someone else."

Abner got to his feet but bent to brush a kiss across Anke's forehead, careless of Aenti Fern. Then he left the room, much lighter in heart at the knowledge that Anke would get well. . . .

Anke avoided Aenti Fern's knowing eyes as she sipped a cup of beef broth.

"That man's *narrisch* about ya, Anke."

"It doesn't matter. It would never work."

Aenti Fern sniffed. "Let me tell ya a story about never working. . . . *Gott* decides if it'll work. I remember walkin' ta the school *haus* when I wuz about ten. I had found a beautiful butterfly—bright blue and yellow—and I wanted ta bring it in ta show the class. I didn't know enough ta understand that me touchin' those *wunderbaar* wings would be enough ta destroy its power ta fly. A mean *maedel* named Barbara *kumme* along and mocked me, told me I killed the butterfly. She said I might as well have jest stepped on it right there. I started ta cry, and Barbara laughed. But then I opened my hand and the beautiful creature flew off, right above our heads. I learned that day that a lie can't keep somethin' from bein' free. That butterfly flew, and *Gott* shut Barbara's mouth. Ya need ta believe that *Gott* can shut the mouth of yer past and whatever it is that ya got held so tight within ya. Ya got ta live fer today and not fer the times when somebody broke yer wings. Ya trust *Gott* and ya can still fly. Believe me."

Anke's hand shook as she held her cup and she let the tears fall freely from her eyes. "*Danki*, Aenti Ruth. That's the best medicine you could give me. And I'll try; I'll try."

Chapter Thirty-One

The first chill of autumn came to Blackberry Falls, but the sun still shone brightly, and it was a *gut* day for the community to *kumme* together to build the cabin for Tabitha and Matthew. After the two deaths of Amy and *Frau* Smucker, it was healing to gather to celebrate new marriage rather than to mourn.

Tabitha had told no one but her friend Abigail about her plans to work on the cabin by lamplight. But, for the moment, she dutifully helped Anke, who was working more slowly after being ill.

Working alongside the other women, they were making slow-cooked molasses and baked beans, as well as large casseroles of scalloped potatoes. Hams had been smoked and baked to feed the men at noontime, and there would also be hot roast beef for sandwiches and a large assortment of pumpkin pies and desserts.

All the food was to be transported by wagon to the site of the new home. As Tabitha was helping to carry things outside, she was surprised to see her *daed* near the back porch. He was standing as if he were in great thought and Tabitha hesitantly approached him.

"Da, are you all right?"

"Tabby . . . hmm . . . *jah*, just came back to get my favorite screwdriver."

She accepted his answer, but something bothered her about his expression. "Is anything worrying you?" she asked, reaching out to touch his sleeve.

He patted her hand absently, then looked down into her eyes. "I'm fine, *kind*. I was thinking how much you look like your *mamm*. She was beautiful, Tabby, as you are."

"*Danki*, Daed."

"It will not be the same to have you away from home— for all that I begged you to marry. I never really considered that you'd have your own cabin."

His sad smile tugged at her heart. "It's only a half mile away, Da. And I will see you often."

He seemed to perk up at her words. "Of course you will. I'm only being foolish. And soon there will be *kinner* to *kumme* and visit as well."

Tabitha felt herself flush as she agreed with a smile. In truth, she wondered how soon there might be grandchildren when she and Matthew had not even consummated their marriage. Yet she was confident that the raising of their own cabin would bring them more time alone together, and she felt in her heart that she was beginning to know and understand her husband better.

She shook off her thoughts as her *daed* walked away, and she went to help Anke carry a few last bottles of homemade root beer to the food wagon. Then they drove to the site.

Tabitha nodded to herself when they arrived, pleased

to see the outer walls of the cabin framed and up in good order.

She had wanted nothing elaborate when it came to the new home. She'd been raised in rather grand rooms but here desired simplicity, and Matthew had agreed.

She caught sight of him, standing tall and handsome, with the wind playing in his chestnut hair. He was holding a hammer and was clearly listening to something Big Jim was saying. It thrilled her to think that Matthew was her husband, and she picked her way carefully through the construction materials to tap him lightly on the shoulder.

He turned, and when he caught sight of her, he bent and *bussed* her quickly on the mouth.

"Hello, my pretty."

Tabitha felt herself blush with his praise. *It's a funny thing, because others have complimented me and yet none of them bear remembering since Matthew has* kumme *into my life.*

Something of her thoughts must have communicated to him because he encircled her with one strong arm and bent to whisper in her ear, "Soon you'll be working on the wood, as is your right, Tabitha."

She nodded, wanting to tell him how much she appreciated his words, but she stepped away lightly when she saw Big Jim looking at them.

"I won't keep you from your work."

As she walked away, she realized that she wanted to show Matthew her secret workshop. Distracted, she nearly ran full tilt into Christi.

Tabitha laughed as she set the young girl on her feet.

"I'm sorry, Christi. I bet you're wanting to see the wood-working up close."

"*Jah* . . . but Mamm says I need ta help with the dishes."

"Well," Tabitha encouraged, "so do I for the moment. Let's *geh* help together."

"Every cabin needs a little front porch ta sit on," Big Jim commented to Matthew.

Matthew nodded. "Someplace to sit and rock the *kinner* when they can't sleep."

"For a newly married man, ya have great insight, Matt. There wuz many a time when I had ta rock Christi ta sleep as a *boppli* when she wuz teethin'."

"I look forward to times like those."

Matthew carefully knocked a nail into place in the porch frame, then took a deep breath of air redolent with the smell of fresh pinewood. Curled shavings of wood fell to the ground like fragrant snow as men worked on the upper beams and roof.

"Ach, young Matthew . . . how do ya like your cabin so far?" Bishop Kore asked, coming up behind him.

"It's *gut*, sir. Just right for us."

"A bit removed from the general community, though," the bishop observed.

"We wanted it that way."

"*Jah*, it's *gut* to have some time apart from others. Though you will have the field mice . . . the termites . . . the ants. . . . the bats . . . the ladybugs, the spiders, and—"

Matthew nodded politely before the bishop could *geh* on. "*Jah*, sir . . . all of those. *Danki* for your blessing. If you'll excuse me, I'm going to see what else I can do to help Big Jim."

"*Jah* . . . of course. *Geh* on . . . I'll test the ground for the termites. Save ya some work later on. Ach, and I'll have a word with the bats. You know some miss the dawn and hang about during the day."

Matthew watched the man wander off and wondered once more how it was possible for the bishop to be so gifted at church meeting but so odd in the every day.

"Still, each man has his own path . . . " Matthew muttered under his breath, then turned to resume working with Big Jim.

Abner knelt on the ground with his blue shirtsleeves rolled up to his forearms. He plunged his hands into the bucket of soapy water and got cleaned up for lunch. But even as he wiped his neck and face, his sole focus was Anke. He could tell that she was tired and that she'd lost some weight from her illness. He longed to see her wan cheeks full of roses and her waist as pleasantly curved as always.

But for now, he'd be happy just to talk with her. She'd become rather withdrawn since she was sick and he'd had little chance to see her alone.

He walked over to the movable church benches, which had been covered and loaded with food. He took a plate and some silverware and made his way down the line, barely noticing what he scooped up until he came to Anke, who presided over a giant pan of scalloped potatoes.

"Anke—how are ya? I—I've thought about you a lot since ya was ill."

He ignored the teenaged *Amisch buwe* behind him, who clearly cared only to keep the line moving past the potatoes.

"I'm fine, Abner. Fine."

"Well, uh . . . how about—"

"You're holdin' up the line, Abner," she said bluntly.

Something inside him snapped. "I don't care, Anke. But since ya don't care neither, I'll keep movin' on."

He regretted his words as soon as they were out of his mouth, especially when, farther down the line, the Widow Miller laid an extra slice of ham on his plate.

"Hiya, Abner. I heard what ya said ta Anke." She laughed gaily. "Why not try some supper at my *haus* one evening? I promise ta keep the meal . . . hot."

Abner felt the back of his neck grow warm. He wasn't used to such brazen talk, especially when Anke was within earshot.

He mumbled a reply, then quickly went on to the sweet potatoes and *auld Frau* Umble, who was easily over ninety. She slapped a spoonful on his plate and gave him a birdlike glare from her dark eyes. "Abner Mast, don't listen ta such foolishness! Ya don't need a woman, jest a quick dip in the creek!"

By now he wanted to sink under the bench, but he nodded respectfully instead. "Uh, *jah. Danki*, ma'am."

He fled the serving line and wandered aimlessly to an empty picnic blanket under a nearby oak tree, wishing he could be anywhere else. . . .

Anke miserably ladled out scalloped potatoes in an absent fashion. She'd been surprised and then hurt by

Abner's words, *Since ya don't care neither . . . But I do care. It's just that you deserve better than soiled goods.*

Then she felt *Gott* speak to her heart. *You are my child and there is nothing that has happened in the past that can change the good plans I have for your future. Nothing that I cannot turn to bless your life.*

The thought was completely alien to her and she felt herself trying to reject it. *If Gott wanted my life to be gut, why did He allow my* oncle *to do what he did to me? Why, when I was but a child?*

The thought made tears fill her eyes and she abandoned the scalloped potatoes to turn and run blindly into the woods. She ran for a long time before finally dropping to the ground, exhausted, on a soft bed of moss.

Chapter Thirty-Two

Abner finished his food and was preparing to *geh* back to work on the cabin when he noticed that Anke was no longer serving. He thought she had gone to eat with the other women and let his gaze sweep over the various picnic blankets. Finally, he walked back to the serving bench, where *auld Frau* Umble caught his eye and motioned him over. He went rather unwillingly until he heard the woman speak.

"If yer lookin' fer Anke, she ran off into the woods. Looked like she was cryin' too. I tell ya, Abner, women are trouble. The creek would do ya better."

"*Danki*," he muttered, then bent to *buss* her cheek. He ignored her pleased gasp of surprise and headed for the forest.

It was fairly easy to track Anke's path—a broken stick here, a crushed flower there—but when he finally came to the mossy haven she had found, he discovered that she was sound asleep.

She had flung an arm over her eyes as a child might do and her dress and apron were askew. Her brown curls had come loose from her *kapp* and fell about her in a manner only her husband should have the privilege of seeing. Abner knew this and was humbled by the vision.

He crept close to her and dropped to his knees, gently lifting a curl of her hair and pressing it to his lips. Her hair smelled fresh and clean and faintly like lilacs, and he was more than content to simply sit by her, waiting until she awoke.

When she did move her arm from her face he saw that her cheeks were tearstained, and his heart ached for her. Her long, dark lashes fluttered open and she stared up at him, clearly caught in that place between sleep and wakefulness.

"Abner? Ach . . . Abner."

He couldn't help himself; he bent to kiss her, at first meaning only to brush her lips with his own. But then he felt her tentatively respond and it set his blood on fire.

He lay down next to her on the mossy ground with a groan, kissing the sweet curve of her neck. She arched her back, giving him better access, but then he felt her stiffen and *kumme* wide awake.

"Abner—what?"

He pulled away and sat up, putting his elbows on his knees and his head in his hands. "I'm sorry," he muttered.

"Abner, what is it?"

"Kissin' ya, not kissin' ya. I'm worn out with it, Anke."

"Well—"

He heard the huffiness in her voice and quickly lifted his head. "Anke, I don't mean it that way. . . . I jest want ya to know . . . that I love ya." He caught her hands in his and looked down at her careworn fingers, not wanting to see her reaction to how he truly felt.

"Abner . . ." This time her voice was soft and sweet, and he looked up to meet her brown eyes. "Ach, Abner. . . . I love ya too. But if ya really knew about me, ya wouldn't want me in yer life."

"Try me, *sei se gut*. Please try me and trust me. I will hold whatever ya tell me close and dear to my heart. I give ya my word."

Anke stared up into his earnest blue eyes, and her thoughts drifted back to when she was but a child. "My *oncle*—he was—often left alone to watch me. I don't know what my *mamm* was thinking, but after my *daed* died, she had ta work, and entrusted me ta her oldest *bruder*'s care. He . . . always made me feel special somehow. He bought me candies and held my hand. . . . But then . . . then things became different. I was ten years *auld* that year and I was so ignorant, or maybe innocent. He began ta want ta play games with me that I knew were wrong. . . ." She swallowed hard. "And I let him touch me and he hurt me, but I still didn't tell my *mamm*. . . . I should have. It wuz my fault for not tellin'—"

She broke off when she felt what she thought were raindrops hitting her face, and then she blinked and realized that Abner was crying.

"Don't cry, Abner."

He drew a hoarse breath. "I'm cryin' for ya, Anke, that ya have had ta carry the thought that it was yer fault. . . .

more detail. He was an artist's dream, she mused. His long, dark lashes lay in thick crescents on his sleep-flushed cheeks and his perfect lips were parted slightly with his even breathing. His white shirt had come partially undone and the long line of his lean throat was exposed. His right leg was bent and one long-fingered hand rested with negligent strength on his knee. He was quite simply, she thought, irresistible.

Suddenly, as if drawn by invisible cords to him, she put down her wood chisel with quiet care and then crawled across the short distance to the sprawl of his legs. She settled herself, then leaned forward and ran the tip of her tongue across his bottom lip. *It's like licking cream*, she thought, indulging herself once more. She pressed her mouth against the dampness she'd created and kissed him until she felt a groan reverberate in his chest.

His lashes lifted slowly, seemingly with reluctance, and she felt his mouth curve upward in a smile. She drew back and felt him give her a long, heated glance. She was about to speak when a long, whinnied cry rent the *nacht* air.

"That's a horse in pain," Tabitha said, rising to her feet.

"I agree." He too got to his feet, and she felt a warm sensation in her belly when he took her hand and grabbed up one of the lanterns. "Let's *geh*."

She hurried with him through the chill air and felt her heart begin to pound when she heard the horse's cry again. . . .

Matthew suspected that the horse was a mare in labor. He'd heard that same high-pitched cry several times back

It weren't, Anke. . . . It weren't." He cradled h
and she could feel his heart slamming in his che

"I—I felt *Derr Herr* speak ta my heart today.
why I ran."

"What did He say?"

"That He can turn the bad past ta *gut* in my life. I t
I just couldn't believe that until ya *kumme* along and
I told ya. It felt like spring water runnin' through n
Abner—ta tell ya the truth."

"*Danki*, Anke," he whispered hoarsely. "And if there'
more *gut* ta *kumme* out of this, we'll find it—together."

She felt him gently kiss her forehead, and then she
wrapped her arms about his broad shoulders, taking joy
in the idea of togetherness.

The late-*nacht* hum of the crickets and the deep-toned
voice of an *auld* bullfrog were the perfect accompaniment
for the work of carving as far as Tabitha was concerned.
Lightning bugs blinked out a show and she found herself
humming softly so as not to wake Matthew, who half
dozed, sitting up in a corner. They were in their new living
area and it was after midnight. The cabin had been put up
in one day, with many hands making light work. But there
was still the finishing to do, and Tabitha relished the craft.

Still, her eyes were repeatedly drawn from the wood
to the handsome face of her husband in repose. His chestnut hair had grown long of late, and she considered the
intimate pleasure of being able to give him a haircut on
their own porch.

Matthew stirred slightly, causing her to study him in

home. He hurried his steps down a slight hill, careful to make sure that Tabitha kept her footing.

He lifted the lantern when he spotted the horse just ahead. He inched closer with Tabitha at his back. Generally, mares preferred to give birth at *nacht* and in solitude, if possible, but they were usually quiet. This mare was in obvious distress, with her sides heaving and her breathing forced.

"It's breech, I bet," Tabitha whispered.

"Jah, we'll have to be careful approaching her. Do you know this horse?"

"It's Asa Zook's mare, Bunny."

Asa Zook? Matthew flashed back to the day Asa had called him a hex and then left the mill and Blackberry Falls with his *bruder. If his horse is here, then surely Asa is too.* It was a grim thought, but right now he had to focus on the mare.

He let *geh* of Tabitha's hand and slid the few remaining pins from his shirt so he could lower his suspenders. "I'll use my shirt as a harness of sorts. We have to keep her moving after we check her."

"Let me do it, Matthew."

"*Nee*, she might kick."

His wife's delicate laughter rang out in soft tones. "Don't you remember the ad, Mail-Order Groom? You must 'love horses'? That's because I love them and know how to handle them."

She proved her point by walking slowly to the mare and gentling her with low crooning. Then she made a slight motion, and he came forward to lift the lantern.

"It is breech," she said in a worried voice.

"We've got to keep her walking. If she goes down, we'll never be able to turn the foal."

"And I don't think we should *geh* for help. She may try to deliver at any time now," Tabitha pointed out.

Matthew nodded. The terribly difficult thing about a breech presentation was the actual turning of the foal. It took both strength and gentleness, as well as precise timing. He'd only managed it once before, with a silky black horse at home. But he'd been lucky.

"I think we should pray." The words were out of his mouth before he knew it, but then he smiled in the shadows. "Remember what you said in the ad, Tabitha? *Gott* is the recognized third in a marriage. Well, I believe that, and we sure need His strength here tonight."

"*Jah*," he heard her softly agree.

Then he began to pray as he eased his shirt over the mare's neck. "*Derr Herr*, give us strength in this moment to help one of Your creatures and her *boppli*, so that no life may be lost here tonight. . . ."

Matthew felt a strange peace *kumme* over him then, and the following hours seemed to play out easily, as if Someone else guided the watch. . . . The mare had quieted after many a trip around the grassy clearing, and finally dawn began to stretch its pink fingers across the everlightening sky. He joined Tabitha and carefully pushed the foal back far enough to be able to turn its thin legs and bring its head into proper position. After that, they stood gratefully and watched as the mare delivered at last.

"She's marvelous," Tabitha said, watching with him as the new mother licked her *boppli* clean.

Matthew glanced down at his wife. She'd lost her *kapp* and her hair hung in damp tangles over her shoulders and down her back. Her apron was unspeakably soiled, and the hem of her dress was ripped and the color of mud. Still, he had never found her more beautiful. . . . He had seen her fierceness and determination to save both the mare and the foal and her tireless effort over the past hours.

"You're marvelous," he said quietly, bending to kiss her in the new light of day. . . .

Chapter Thirty-Three

"We're courtin'," Abner announced with quiet dignity.

John Stolfus turned to look up from reading *The Budget*, and Abner felt the weight of his stare. "You and Anke?" There was slight disbelief in his question.

"*Jah*. Ya betcha."

The two men were in the Stolfus living area, sitting near a warm fire in the chill of the early morning.

"Well, that's fine, Abner."

"*Danki*. I jest wanted ya ta know, so ya can start lookin' fer someone else ta help around the *haus*. I'd like Anke to keep our own home one day."

Abner watched as his friend , half bruder,and employer nodded affably. *It feels* gut *ta say it out loud. . . . We're courtin'. . . . I love her. . . .*

He was stirred from his thoughts as Anke herself bustled into the room with a tray of tea. She had a shy look on her face and served him before he could even get to his feet.

John cleared his throat after a moment. "I'll see you two later in church meeting. I think I'll *geh* over and check whether Tabby and Matt are getting ready to come. . . . Congratulations!"

He left the room, and Abner stood and sidestepped the small table in front of his chair. Anke had turned away from him slightly to face the fire. "John congratulated us. . . . So, ya told him about our courtin'?"

"*Jah*. I know that most couples court in secret, but Anke—I want *der weldt* ta know. I—I suppose I should have asked ya first."

"*Nee*. It's strange, that be all. Here I am, an *auld* maid, and I'm courtin'." She laughed a little. "I've never courted before," she admitted.

"Well, you're courtin' now, and I am goin' ta try and share with ya every enjoyable moment. And Anke—I'll share the sad times too. I love ya." He felt awkward for a moment when she simply stared up at him and wondered if he'd mentioned love again too soon. . . .

Anke stood, listening for a minute to the negative voice that ran rampant in her head—the voice that said he would leave her eventually, hurt her heart, or *kumme* to hate her as her *oncle* said he did after. . . .

Then she heard a new Voice, that of *Derr Herr*, telling her that Abner was no such man. He was strong, both physically and spiritually, and she knew that he meant what he said. . . . *He loves me. . . . He loves me. . . .*

"I—I don't know what it is ta love a man, Abner, but I know that I feel about ya as I've never felt about anybody before . . . and I—I'm blessed by yer love and patience."

She watched him carefully, wondering how he'd take her words, but then he caught her hands in his and bent to kiss her. "*Danki*, Anke. What ya say is a gift and a blessin' ta me also."

She nodded, the practical side of her remembering the time. "Ach, we'd better hurry ta church, Abner. We're sure ta be late."

He laughed. "Then we'll be late together."

She had to smile up at him as his blue eyes sparkled in the light of the fire, and she decided that being late together sounded rather fun.

Tabitha shivered as she dressed hastily after washing in the nearby creek, which ran from Blackberry Falls. She fixed her *kapp* in place and was glad to peek outside to see Bunny and her new foal resting quietly. Matthew had gone off to bathe himself.

Tabitha felt restless waiting for Matthew to return and decided she might gather her tools, which were still near the bookshelf she'd been carving last *nacht*. She knew it wasn't *gut* to work on a Sunday, but she noticed a slight unevenness in the frame and gently ran a plane over the surface.

"Stop!"

The unfamiliar roar of her *fater*'s voice caused her to jump, and she nearly dropped the plane.

"Fater, I'm sorry!" she exclaimed. "I wasn't meaning to work today."

"Put down that tool now."

There was an eerie soberness about her *fater*'s face, and for some strange reason, she felt a moment of fear as she carefully lowered the plane to the floor.

"Fater, what—"

"Close your lips, Tabitha. You will accompany me to church meeting now and be glad that I don't drag you there by your hair."

"By my hair? Fater, are you well?"

He walked toward her, then caught her arm in an iron grip. "I am well enough to see when my own *dochder* is woodworking!"

"I should have said something, *jah*, but—"

He shook her briefly, then marched her across the freshly sanded floor. "We will *geh* to church meeting and you will confess your sins there."

Tabitha felt as if she was in a strange dream that was fast turning into a nachtmare. She hurried to keep pace with her *fater* and hoped that Matthew would return soon.

Matthew came back from the creek whistling, pleased to see Bunny and her foal doing well and completely absorbed in each other. He entered through the back door of the new *haus* and saw Tabitha's damp tracks on the floor. He smiled at the small size of her feet, then called out for his wife.

When he got no response he walked through the cabin, toweling his hair. As he realized that Tabitha was gone, fear started to flood his body. He dropped the towel, pulled on his shirt, and raised his suspenders. The thought of Amy Dienner's murderer possibly having Tabitha was terrifying. Then he told himself to settle down. She might simply have gone to her *daed*'s or started off to church meeting without him.

He ran the short half mile to the Stolfus *haus* but found no one there, then headed to the Miller barn, where service was being held. He saw Abner and Anke slip inside ahead of him, then hurried to enter the barn himself. He had barely slid the door closed when he became aware of a tense silence inside the space.

He turned to find the strange sight of Tabitha standing in front of the community, her chin up and a bewildered, frightened look on her face. John Stolfus and Bishop Kore stood to her right, and Matthew noticed that Abner and Anke stood frozen in one of the aisles ahead.

Matthew wasted no time moving past Abner and making his way to the front of the community. "What's going on?" he asked loudly. "Tabitha?" He took his wife's cold hand in his and stared out at the troubled faces in front of him. "Bishop Kore?"

But it was John Stolfus who answered, in a tone of voice Matthew had never heard him use before.

"I caught Tabitha in the act of working wood! I brought her here to confess her sins before the community. She refuses to speak, and if she continues to so choose, she shall be shunned."

"Shunned," Matthew repeated incredulously. Matthew had never in his life witnessed a shunning, and he was amazed to hear his *fater*-in-law speak so coldly about it.

"*Jah*," John bit out. "She is worse than a hex to dare to work with wood—and I am ashamed to have caught her just as I once discovered her mother."

Matthew ignored the gasps of the onlookers as John's words about Tabitha's *mamm* flooded his mind. He turned and saw the stricken look on Tabitha's face.

"My *mamm*?" she asked, gazing at her *fater*. "You mean before she died?"

Matthew could see the arrow coming, the hard truth

that would pierce Tabitha's heart. He could do nothing to stop it except—

"I am the one who encouraged Tabitha to try woodworking. I told her to do it—as her husband. So the blame is mine." He heard his own voice ring out with strength and conviction. And he succeeded in turning Tabitha's attention from her *fater* for the moment, though he knew he could not protect her from the truth forever.

Chapter Thirty-Four

"I thought it would be a lot less fun to be shunned," Matthew commented with an attempt at cheerfulness. He and Tabitha were hiking up the mountain above Blackberry Falls. They both had been officially banned after the wood-carving debacle that morning.

He glanced back to see that his wife's beautiful face was still stained with tears and he tightened his jaw, wishing he could do something to help her. Her *fater*, now that they were under "the *bann*," would not speak to her, so there was no opportunity to discover anything more about her *mamm* and wood carving.

Matthew had helped Tabitha to pack a few belongings from their new home, including the carved ladle, and they had left Bunny and her foal in the small pasture, where Bishop Kore had promised to keep them safe until Asa Zook could be found. Matthew knew that shunning could look different from *Amisch* community to community. For example, many *Amisch* practiced shunning by allowing the shunned person to continue living in the community even while they were completely ignored. The shunned could not eat or sleep with their family until they had repented of their sin and the community deemed them worthy to return to normal life. But, apparently, in Blackberry Falls, shunned sinners were sent into the forest to live a makeshift life in an *auld* hunting cabin at the head of the falls.

"It's what the *Englisch* would call a 'time-out' cabin!" he said, trying once more to lighten Tabitha's mood, but her face remained somber when he glanced back at her.

Finally, they emerged on the top of the rather treacherous but beautiful cliff face.

"The cabin's over there," Tabitha said dully.

Matthew caught her hand in his. "Then let's *geh* see our new abode."

The cabin truly was ramshackle in appearance. It was rectangular and made of gray, sagging wood. A few small windows with crooked frames seemed to look out bleakly on the world, and the front steps appeared completely lethal.

"Whew! What a place. . . . When was the last time somebody was shunned?"

"Not for years," Tabitha responded.

"I can tell. Still, there are certain advantages to being shunned . . . alone . . . together." He let his voice lower suggestively, but he barely earned a smile from her.

Then he stopped walking and turned to put his hands on her slender shoulders. "I know you're thinking about your *mamm* and what your *fater* said. . . . Do you—remember anything about her?"

"*Nee*—I was only a young *boppli* when she died." She looked up at him, her sapphire-blue eyes wide. "I suppose that if she was doing woodwork and Fater discovered her, it must have been before I was born. From the way he was talking today, surely she must have been shunned?"

"I know you have more questions than answers, and I want to help you if I can. Abner revealed to me a piece of the mystery surrounding your mother. He said that the carved wooden ladle was given as a gift to you at the request of your *mamm*. He also said that your mother was one of the best wood carvers he'd ever seen."

"Abner knows? What else did he say?"

Matthew shook his head. "He said something about you and I having to work out the mystery ourselves."

"I've always loved that ladle, felt that it had some special importance, but I assumed that it had been a gift from my *fater*."

"Maybe when this shunning is over, we can talk with your *daed* and get some answers."

She gave him a grateful look that melted his heart. "I like how you say 'we' can talk with him. I thought he had lost his mind this morning."

"He was angry. . . . Perhaps he could not control your *mamm* or her talent, and he feared the same thing would happen with you."

"I am so grateful that you appreciate my carving. Someday soon I would love to show you my workshop," she added shyly.

He bent and kissed her slowly. "I'd love a tour—I would love seeing anything that matters to your heart."

Abner knew that Anke was beside herself with worry for Tabitha, and he planned to do something to ease her mind. He entered the Stolfus kitchen to find her listlessly wiping the table.

"How are ya?" he asked softly, unsure of where John might be.

Anke lifted sorrow-filled brown eyes to him and shook her head. "It's happening all over again, isn't it? John is full of fear and judgment and loss, I think. He will send Tabitha away if she does not confess and repent."

Abner put his hands on her soft shoulders. "You don't know that, and perhaps she will confess soon."

"*Nee*, it's in her blood—the wood. She won't be able ta stay away from it."

Abner sighed. "All right, but we can do nothing now. So, I want ya ta *kumme* with me on a walk."

"Ach, but I must start supper soon."

"John can eat leftovers. Now, *kumme, sei se gut*."

"All right."

He took her hand in a firm grip and led her through the screen door and down the porch steps. Then he walked with her away from the cabin and the other homes until they'd reached the communal apple orchards. There was no one about and he slowed his pace so that they both could breathe in the ripe scent of the apples that would soon be ready for harvest.

"It's nice here," Anke said softly. "Usually I only *kumme* to the orchard to work in the fall."

"Anke, I—I know we just started courtin', but there are things I wish for ya now."

"Like what?"

"Well, that ya wouldn't have ta work so hard, for starters."

She seemed to be thinking about his words and he waited patiently for her response.

"I guess the deep down truth is that I've always worked

hard, ever since . . . I suppose I worked ta keep from thinking about what happened ta me."

He reached to gently stroke her cheek. "But ya don't have ta try and outrun it anymore, Anke. Ya can learn ta be still with the truth, still with *Gott*, mebbe still with me. Ya don't have ta fear the past no more; I'll see it through with ya."

She nodded, reaching into the collar of her dress for her white hankie as a tear spilled from her pretty eyes.

"*Danki*, Abner. Ya give me peace."

He smiled, feeling his heart expand with gratitude, and he silently thanked *Derr Herr* for the privilege of loving Anke.

Tabitha swept the dusty floor with vigor and made herself sneeze in the process.

"You sneeze like a mouse," Matthew offered from where he stood in the open doorway of the cabin.

She stopped her sweeping and smiled at him. "This is actually a bit fun. We can pretend we're new settlers to Blackberry Falls." She wondered if he'd find her fancy immature. But he came forward and took her in his arms. Broom and all.

"I like your idea of play. If we are new settlers, can you tell me, my *gut* wife, how many *kinner* we should pretend we have?"

"Ach—" She waved her hand airily. "Why not six?"

"Mmm . . . and do you recall if we . . . had fun in their making?"

She felt her eyes drawn to his fine mouth and nodded. "*Jah*," she whispered. She stretched on tiptoe to give him a sultry kiss and he responded in kind, leaving her breathless.

Suddenly, the atmosphere in the *auld* cabin became quite heated, and Tabitha felt herself let *geh* of the broom to link her arms about his neck. She kissed him in a way she never had before, creating a tumult in her own body. She wanted them to be man and wife in truth.

"Ach, Matthew . . ."

He bent and swept her up into his arms, walking over to the makeshift rope bed they'd restrung that afternoon. The mattress was thin and the bedstead creaked, but she knew that it was strong enough to support their combined weight. She watched him pull carelessly at the pins in his shirt and heard the small tinkling sound as they hit the floor. She was helping to ease his shirt off his shoulders when a gruff voice called out from the doorway.

"Hello! Anyone about?"

Tabitha suppressed a sigh and didn't miss the groan that reverberated through Matthew's chest.

He quickly shrugged his shirt back on and pulled her up from the bed. She turned and peered through the filtered light of the dusty room to see Asa Zook standing in the doorway.

Matthew immediately felt protective of Tabitha and stepped in front of her before walking out of the cabin.

"Zook, we're shunned here, so we don't need anyone about."

"I know all about the shunning. The bishop told me, and he also told me that Bunny's foal was breech and ya saved the two of them. I *kumme* ta give ya my thanks and ta bring ya some supplies."

Matthew was conscious of Tabitha standing on the steps behind him, and he nodded briefly at Asa, then reached to accept the sack of goods the other man held out.

"I thought you left the mill and Blackberry Falls for *gut*," Matthew said.

"I'm here and there," Asa said gruffly. "I can make my way without the mill well enough."

Matthew nodded, not wanting to prolong the conversation. "*Danki* for the supplies." *And for stopping me from making love to my wife . . .*

He was glad when Asa left with a brief wave.

Chapter Thirty-Five

Autumn came in earnest to Blackberry Falls over the following days, and the trees were a riot of color and scent.

Anke was busy canning and barely saw John Stolfus, even for meals. Since the shunning, he'd been remote and irritable, often walking the woods for hours and neglecting the mill. But Anke had her own worries about Tabitha and her husband and found she had no heart to bring the matter up with John.

"How many jars of wild cherries is that?" Abner asked wryly as he came in the back door of the kitchen.

She shook her head at him. "Twenty-four or so. You know I have ta do this, Abner. It would be a waste not to. Besides, it ain't like real work."

"Oh, it's real work, but I think I might know of a way ta make it more fun."

She eyed him skeptically as he rounded the kitchen counter and grabbed a cherry from the colander in the sink.

"Do you know," he asked softly, "that I absolutely love wild cherries? I lived on them growing up."

"I know ya ran wild in the woods, Abner. I'm sorry ya were forced ta live off the land at such a young age."

"Don't be sorry," he said, moving closer. "It made me strong."

She felt warm and flustered by his nearness, but she couldn't deny that it also felt *gut*. "I'd better get back ta my canning."

"Fine, but first I'd like to ask for a kiss—and I wonder if you would like one too, sweet Anke?"

"I—"

"Please," he whispered.

She couldn't deny that a kiss from Abner was something she badly wanted at that moment. She looked up into his ice-blue eyes and leaned up to brush his lips with her own. He reached his great arms to pull her close and she felt safe and secure as she listened to the thrumming beat of his heart. Then he put her gently from him and she watched, fascinated, as he took the cherry he'd stolen from the bowl and popped it into his mouth. He gave her a faintly wicked smile, and she shivered in excitement as he pulled her close once more.

"Mmm, Anke, the cherry juice is sweet and sour; kiss me again and add ta its sweetness."

Intrigued by his suggestion, she did as he asked. His lips tasted of wild cherry and she surprised herself by reaching to run the tip of her tongue over him, longing to taste more of the juice. And his moan told her instantly that he was more than happy to give her exactly what she wanted.

Matthew watched Tabitha carefully as she carved with a small pocketknife. Beneath her capable hands, the stick of beechwood turned from forest-floor debris into the form of a bent *auld* man, walking with a cane. She handed the carving to him shyly.

"It's *wunderbaar*, Tabitha," he praised.

She shrugged her slender shoulders. "It's what I saw in the wood."

He noticed the slight note of sadness in her voice. "You miss your *fater*?"

"I miss the man I thought he was. He just seemed so angry and violent when he saw me carving at the cabin."

"You reminded him of your *mamm*, maybe—a woman woodcarver."

He watched her stroke her carving with a delicate but capable finger. He closed his hand over hers. "We'll find out the truth about your mother, Tabitha. Together."

"*Danki*," she whispered.

He watched the emotions play across her beautiful face and decided that he should ask the question that had been beating about his brain. "Not that I don't love living in this hideaway with you alone, but I wondered what your thoughts are about going back."

She stared at him. "You mean confessing and repenting? I can't, but if you—"

"*Nee*, that's not what I meant. I just thought that you might want to talk about it."

He watched her draw a deep breath. "If I confessed, I wouldn't feel right about doing my woodworking in secret anymore. I mean, I know I've gone against the Ordnung already, but to lie to our people and in church meeting . . . I can't."

"I understand," he soothed. "I wonder, though, how it came about that women aren't allowed to carve wood here. I know in my community back home it wasn't an issue, and even here, Abigail works with clay."

Her lovely brow wrinkled in thought. "I'm not sure, but there must be some reason why Abigail is permitted by Bishop Kore to work with clay."

"We could always move back to my hometown, Renova," he joked.

"You're smiling," she said. "But is there any part of you that would like to *geh* back? I guess I was pretty selfish in my ad—insisting that you give up your home for here."

He bent and kissed the tip of her nose. "I want to be where you are, sweetheart, and I'm happy being your mail-order groom. Besides, Renova was not all that its name implies."

"Really?"

"Yep. You see, my *daed* was bitter after my *mamm*'s death and was a difficult man to deal with, to say the least."

"Like my *daed* is being now?"

He nodded his head slowly. "I guess we have to learn, sooner or later, that the *daeds* we've known were people just like us at our age, with similar cares. I suppose we only see the shadow of who they've been and more of who they are now."

"That's wise," she said, smiling at him.

"We make a *gut* pair, then: wise and far wiser."

"I love you, Matthew."

He saw the shy blush on her fair cheeks and knew a warmth in his heart. "I love you too, *mei frau. . . .*"

* * *

Abner discovered that there were certain advantages to courting outright. Normally, an *Amisch* courtship would happen under cover of *nacht*, but not for him and Anke, and he was happy for this. For one thing, older women stopped looking at him as a prospective husband—he was tired of being pursued by Betsy Shiner and her chicken-feathered *kapp*. He also had the distinct privilege of being able to touch Anke's hand, help her with the chores she insisted on doing, and swiping an occasional kiss from her sweet lips. It was all more than he had ever dreamed he might have in his life, especially when he considered his boyhood. . . .

"Where are ya, Abner?"

He shook himself and came back to the moment in John's kitchen where he sat peeling onions for the apple and onion dish that Anke was making for a late dinner.

"Ach, just thinkin'."

"And are those real tears or 'cause of them onions?" Anke queried softly, and he saw her glance at him with a worried expression.

"It's the onions."

"Uh-huh."

"If I'm cryin' at all, it's because I'm grateful—fer ya and fer us."

Anke put down her paring knife and swiped at her own eyes. "Now you've got me doin' it." She sniffed once, then looked at him. "Ya haven't had much love in yer life, have ya, Abner?"

He shook his head and swallowed hard. "*Nee.*"

"Well, we've got ta see what we can do ta make up fer that, don't we?"

He blinked, his mind immediately racing to the physical. *"Jah?"*

"What was yer favorite meal as a *kind*?"

He laughed. "Ya mean what did I wish for when my stomach gnawed at me with hunger?"

She reached to touch his hand. *"Jah*, Abner. What did ya wish for then?"

"I thought I wanted food," he said finally. "I'd look in cabin windows at suppertime—see some folks happy, some sad—but they all had food while I stood outside in the shadows. But I *kumme* ta know that it wasn't the food on the table that mattered. . . . It was the privilege of being able to sit around the table that mattered. John gave me that when he gave me a place here." He looked deep into her soft eyes. "And now you would give it ta me again?"

"Jah, Abner. There will always be a place fer ya beside me."

He put down his head to kiss her fingers, his eyes welling with tears. When she pulled him close to her soft shoulder, he knew a complete feeling of home.

Tabitha looked up from peeling the sweet potatoes that had been among the items Asa Zook had brought. Christi's bright red hair shone beneath her *kapp* in the afternoon sun, rivaling the red of the changing trees.

The *maedel* had a sack slung over one shoulder and appeared anxious. "Where's Matthew?"

"Off fishing. What have you got there?"

"Well, Mamm would have a fit if she knew, but I figured I'd bring ya some tools from the workshop."

"Ach!" Tabitha abandoned the sweet potatoes and

took the sack with a smile. "You're a *schmart* girl, Christi, and a *gut* friend! Won't you *kumme* in to our grand, new haus?"

She led the girl up the newly framed steps and onto the rather treacherous porch. "Only step on every third board, Christi. I haven't yet made all the repairs needed."

She opened the screen door and glanced back to find Christi looking perplexed. "What is it?"

Christi gestured to all the obvious improvements that had been made to the little place. "I know what Matthew said the day you both wuz shunned—that he made you work the wood. But what does he really think? Don't he mind that you, a woman, are better than he at wood-working?"

Tabitha considered the question before she responded. "Christi, it's true that some men would not like that I am more skilled, but Matthew is different somehow. He is confident in himself, and so he can believe in me and my work."

Christi laughed. "I guess *Gott* had you two meet up then, right?"

"You know, my friend, I have never thought of it like that until now, but I couldn't have a better husband than Matthew—even if I had described him myself."

Chapter Thirty-Six

Anke paced before the Stolfus library door, waiting for a word with John. Two weeks had passed and there had been no sign of Tabitha or Matthew coming anywhere near to confessing. The weather was turning colder and Tabitha had always seemed to catch a chest cold in the late autumn ever since she was a child.

Anke was distracted from her worried thoughts by the sight of Abner standing in the archway of the living room. For a big man, he always seemed to move with silent grace, and she couldn't help but admire the strength of his forearms, revealed by his rolled-up blue sleeves.

"Studyin' on me, Anke?" he asked softly, giving her a wicked grin.

"*Nee*," she protested, feeling her cheeks flame.

"Well, I have *nee* problem admittin' that I like ta study yer sweet shape—yer curves are full and soft, jest right ta fit my hands. . . ."

Anke helplessly crossed her arms in front of herself. *How can he make me feel like he's touchin' me when he's across the room?*

He seemed to know that he wove some spell about her that left her unable to move, for he closed the distance between them and took her in his arms. She closed her eyes and waited in delicious expectation for the touch of his lips. However, a brusque "Ahem!" made her eyes fly open and she saw John Stolfus standing in the doorway of the small library.

She stammered a bit, but Abner laughed easily, sliding a big arm around her waist and turning her to face her employer.

"I'm glad somebody's happy," John said sourly.

Anke wanted to reply, but Abner beat her to it. "Ya might be a bit more joyful yerself if ye'd let the past *geh*."

Anke waited for an explosion from John but none came, and she breathed a deep sigh of relief. Perhaps John would listen to *gut* sense after all. . . .

Matthew caught Tabitha's hand in his and pressed it hard against the thin mattress. He was trying desperately to keep a rein on the urgency his body felt but lost more of his control with each breathy sigh she made.

He had been no monk back in his hometown, but never had he felt as he did now, with Tabitha's subtle movements bringing him ever closer to the brink of reason. When he stared down into the passion-washed depths of his wife's blue eyes, he found that she was as caught up in the moment as he was. . . . He heard her soft whisper of pleasure and came apart with her until he lay gasping upon her breast. . . .

"As that was the first time we made love," Matthew

said, smiling, "I'd say that our future will be blessed by the union of ourselves."

He watched her blue eyes sparkle as she reached to brush his hair from his forehead. "I most definitely agree."

Tabitha hummed softly to herself as she carefully scraped out the interior of a dried gourd she'd found in the little *haus*. Her thoughts dwelt on her husband's love-making; those tender, heated kisses and the deep satisfaction her body knew from his. She looked up when she heard a footfall on the porch, not expecting Matthew back from fishing so soon.

"Hiya," she called out gaily, but the smile faded from her lips when the tall, cloaked form made *nee* reply.

Some instinct drew her to her feet as a shiver of fear ran down her spine. She picked up a chisel from the small table in front of her and backed herself against the opposite side of the bed, away from the door.

"What do you want?" She was surprised to hear her own voice quavering in her ears. It felt as though she was a prey animal that had encountered a wounded mountain lion.

"Don't ask me what I want, my beauty. Ask me what I have."

Immediately, her thoughts rushed to Matthew, and whether or not he might have been hurt in some way. She took a death grip on the chisel and straightened her spine. "What do you have, then?"

"That's simple, sweet Tabitha. I have you. . . ."

* * *

Abner stared into John's blue eyes and wondered what his blood kin was thinking. Shunning a *dochder* and new *sohn*-in-law could not be easy, but the past could not be escaped sometimes. Abner knew that John had been drinking heavily and trying to run from his own thoughts, but there came a time when every man must face his torments and choose to turn to *Gott* to bear the problem.

He was still considering how *Derr Herr* might help John when his Anke spoke up boldly.

"John Stolfus, ya must tell your *dochder* the truth. No more lies and hidin'."

"What is the truth?" John asked with bitterness. "That I lost Miriam and now will lose our child?"

"Only if you choose to, John," Abner said quietly.

There was a pause in the conversation and the front door was pushed open with such force that it banged on the wall.

"Tabitha has been taken," Matthew said forcefully as he stalked into the room.

"What are ya sayin', *buwe*?" Abner asked, feeling dread in the pit of his stomach.

"There were signs of a struggle in the small cabin. She fought hard not to *geh*, but I fear the same one who strangled Amy Dienner now has Tabitha."

"What makes you think it's the same person?" John asked, as if rousing himself from a stupor.

"The small eagle that Tabitha carved is gone—missing

from the mantel over the fire. I believe she took it as a sign to me."

"More carvings . . . " Matthew heard John mutter.

"Your *dochder*, sir," Matthew countered.

"I will gather a search party," Abner said, and he was pleased to notice that John made ready to *geh* as well.

Chapter Thirty-Seven

Tabitha had *nee* chance to discover the identity of her abductor; she knew only that he kept her bound behind him and that they were making a merciless trek ever deeper into the mountains. She'd struggled to undo the tight ropes about her wrists but hadn't been able to work the masterful knots.

She had managed to grab the carving of the eagle she had done and slipped it into her apron pocket. She had also succeeded in lashing out and digging her chisel into her captor's forearm, but then he had slapped her calmly, brutally, and she had dropped her makeshift weapon.

She began to grow weary as the trek continued and daylight faded but knew she must keep her wits about her in order to escape. She began to pray beneath her breath, begging *Gott* for support to aid her scratched and bleeding legs. She remembered the Bible verse that promised "that those who wait upon *Derr Herr* shall find new strength . . ." She breathed a sigh of relief when her abductor finally paused in a moonlit clearing, as if considering their direction.

"You'll never hide from *mei* husband," she muttered, her throat parched.

He turned then and eased off his hat and cloak. She looked up with horror as Elam Smucker pulled on the rope that bound her, bringing her inches from his crooked smile. "You are mine now, Tabitha. As you've wanted to be all along. You needn't pretend anymore, nor feign favor for that ruffian who would call you his . . . and, as you asked or pointed out, it is much cozier without my mother." He laughed hoarsely. "See. I have done much for you."

Tabitha swallowed hard. "And Amy Dienner?"

"A whore," he said with a wave of dismissal. "She dared to mock you to my face and she met with an appropriate end."

Tabitha thought desperately of how she might escape and decided that getting Elam to trust her might help. "I see," she said softly. "You have done much for me. Now, allow me to be free of these ropes—that I might—" She swallowed back bile. "That I might repay you with kind hands."

Elam laughed out loud, the sound of one who'd lost his grip on reality, and Tabitha shuddered as he turned and pulled her close once more.

"*Nee*, my beauty, not yet will I loose you. Not until we've climbed the Devil's Elbow—a fitting and secure location for you to watch Matthew King die."

Tabitha knew of the distant peak Elam named. It was patterned with shale stone and deep timber. It would be a fortified location, but she vowed with all her heart that it would be Elam and not Matthew who would meet his end on the dangerous height. . . .

Anke pulled her dark cloak tightly about her and gave Abner a stubborn look. "I be capable of lookin' fer the *maedel* just the same as ya."

She frowned up at him when he leaned in close. "I know that ya love the girl as much as the rest of us, but we must take the horses and ride hard in order ta find a trail."

Anke didn't want to agree with him, though she knew he was probably right. She let him brush her forehead with a discreet kiss, then watched as he turned to John and Big Jim. Bishop Kore held a coil of rope, and even Asa Zook was there, along with his *bruder*. Other men stood outside the Stolfus *haus*, while women circled about, handing out packs of sandwiches and fruit.

When the search party had gone Anke rallied the women together to pray and prepare more food in the Stolfus kitchen. Only then did she slip unnoticed out of the back door and head down to the stables in the cold *nacht* air. . . .

"It's a strange thing—ach, not as strange as burping popcorn—but strange nonetheless."

Matthew looked at Bishop Kore in the moonlit air and wondered what the spiritual leader of Blackberry Falls was talking about. "What's strange?"

Bishop Kore clucked to his horse and then shook his head. "This searching . . . We're searching for a shunned member of our community, who is supposed to be outside our notice. And frankly, I shouldn't be speaking to you either, young Matthew."

Matthew sighed and saw his breath on the air. Shunning to him seemed a futile practice, especially when there was a danger that superseded whatever transgression the person had been shunned for in the first place. "You don't have to speak to me, sir," Matthew said finally.

Bishop Kore smiled. "But I want to . . . there's the rub! I like you, Matthew, and I like you and Tabitha together—like damp noodles."

"Right. But then can you tell me specifically why Tabitha's carving wood was worth shunning her?"

"Ach, but that's not my story to tell."

Matthew sighed heavily. "I've heard this before. If it's not your story, then who—"

"It's my story, *buwe*," John Stolfus interjected hoarsely as he drew abreast of Matthew's horse.

"Then will you tell me, sir—for Tabitha's sake?" Matthew asked.

"*Nee* . . . not until she's found safe. That is what's most important."

"You're right." Matthew nodded. "Let's press on. Huntress sounds as though she's picked up a trail."

Anke leaned forward in the saddle, glad for the company of Aenti Fern, who sat sidesaddle on a pale white horse named Moonlight. The *aulder* woman rode with the ease of a child and gave Anke confidence by her very presence.

Anke wet her lips, then spoke softly into the *nacht*.

"I've known ya ta have the sight, Aenti Fern. Do ya know who it is that took Tabitha?"

"*Jah*—I know this. It be the same man who killed Amy Dienner –I can see his hands, long and thin, bent upon evil. . . ."

Anke shivered in fear for her *maedel* but still was glad that she'd *kumme*. Something in her heart had prompted her night ride and she knew she must obey that still, small Voice.

Tabitha gasped with relief when the ropes around her wrists were untied. Then she looked around the miserable shed of a cabin as Elam turned up a kerosene lamp. There was a ramshackle table and two chairs, as well as an uneven floor littered with cigarette butts.

"Filthy *Englisch*," Elam muttered, swiping his big shoe across the floor. Then Tabitha felt his attention turn to her.

Something of her fear and loathing of him must have shown on her face because he reached an almost tender hand to her cheek. She resisted the urge to shake him off, remembering her plan to get him to trust her.

"Ach, sweet Tabitha, as soon as Matthew King is dead, you and I can be married, as is proper—though I wonder if Bishop Kore is up to the ceremony—a little nutty, wouldn't you say?"

She nodded automatically, understanding now that unlike Bishop Kore, Elam's grasp on reality had fallen away and that she was at the mercy of a madman. She knew that keeping him calm would be another way of gaining his trust, though she shuddered when he withdrew two pistols from his belt and laid them on the table.

She accepted the chair he offered, unsure whether it would bear her weight. Then she folded her hands in her lap, hoping that he would accept her outward calmness as compliance and not tie her up again. Apparently her plan worked because Elam put a satchel on the table next to the guns. He withdrew an apple and handed it to her, seemingly without thought.

She took the fruit and ate it quickly. She had no idea how long she would be held and she needed to keep up her strength. But she knew, glancing out the dark single window of the shack, that *Gott* was looking out for her and that Matthew would surely come. . . .

Abner rode his horse with easy control through a large stand of evergreens. He could hear the howl of Aenti Fern's dog, Huntress, from somewhere in the distance, and he knew that they were gaining ground on whoever it was who'd taken Tabitha.

He pushed away the dark thoughts that whispered they might already be too late, then set his mind to praying. He thought of Anke and prayed for her as well, his heart feeling heavy at leaving her behind.

But then he drew abreast of John, who appeared to have left the *buwe* behind.

"It will be well, John," he offered.

His *auld* friend grunted in response, then spoke softly. "I loved Miriam."

Abner cleared his throat. "I know that."

"But she—she loved the wood more than me. . . ."

"Maybe not, John. I've held my peace for a long time, but maybe—and ya can belt me if I lie—maybe ya drove her off by believin' that lie—that ya were not as important as the carvin'."

To Abner's surprise, John seemed to listen, and then reached out a gloved hand to touch Abner's arm for an instant. "Perhaps you are right, but I cannot undo what I've lost already. . . ."

"*Nee*, but ya can value what ya do have, and it's more than most, John . . . much more than most. . . ."

Chapter Thirty-Eight

Morning dawned gray, cold, and foggy. Tabitha shook herself awake, realizing that she'd fallen asleep upright in her chair. She heard the far-off howling of a dog and tried to blink away the sleepiness from her eyes. She looked about the cabin and found that Elam wasn't there, and that the guns were missing from the table.

She got to her feet cautiously and then tiptoed across the floor. She swallowed a gasp when a gunshot sounded close by, and then Elam appeared in the doorway, an evil grin on his face.

"I do believe, your dear, better-to-be-departed, mistake of a husband will soon be arriving. I just gave them a warning shot, but the Devil's Elbow is merciless terrain. . . . They'll not be able to approach by horse."

All the better—they'll have more chance of cover, she thought. Then an idea came to her, clear and simple. She turned her back on Elam, a calculated move to demonstrate her relaxed attitude, and then resumed her seat at the table.

"You are so sure that marrying Matthew was a mistake— perhaps I'd better explain to you the unusual circumstances of our wedding. . . ."

"You needn't lie to protect the fellow, Tabitha. Don't you remember? I saw the lout in the forest with you, the day of your wedding—"

"*Jah*," she interrupted. "But I'm talking about the particulars of how we met. . . . It involves a rather interesting letter or, um, ad. . . ."

Matthew tied up his mount with the others near a stand of shade trees with plenty of grass. The Devil's Elbow, as the place was called, loomed upward in front of him, and there was no mistaking the sound of a gunshot that pierced the fog. Huntress returned to the party of men but then sniffed the air and ran off in the opposite direction. Matthew frowned. "What does that dog scent?"

"Likely a squirrel for breakfast," Abner replied beside him.

"All right, I'm going to get started," Matthew said, his hand on a coil of rope.

"Wait, *buwe*." Abner put out a bulky arm. "We don't know what we're facing. It might be better if we don't approach from here—the one who fired that gun is expecting us. Maybe we *kumme* around from the back."

"The back of Devil's Elbow." Asa Zook shook his head. "It's all slate. I used to play there as a kid –nearly killed myself."

"We can make it," Matthew said. "We'll *geh* slow."

Asa looked him in the eye. "I once called ya a flat-lander, but it's your wife he's got up there. So I can't deny ya. We'll *geh* slow, as ya say."

"*Danki*," Matthew said clearly, glad that Asa Zook no longer seemed an enemy.

* * *

Abner insisted on going first and, in truth, he was by far the most familiar of the party with mountain travel. He waved Matthew back when he would have gone ahead.

"Wait, *buwe*—Matthew. Ya got a wife up there, a future."

Abner wasn't prepared for the thump to his chest that Matthew responded with. "And what about you, Abner?" the *buwe* whispered. "What about Anke?"

"Ach, *kumme* on. . . . I mean—I know I care for her—"

"You're courting," Matthew persisted. "And in our *weldt*, folks have a funny way of marrying the person they court."

Abner nodded. "All right. Ya climb next ta me and try not ta slide on the slate; it'll make enough noise ta wake the dead."

To make matters more difficult, as the men slowly began the treacherous climb, it began to rain. The slate stone broke off more easily in bad weather, but the sound of the rain disguised the noise of the rocks sliding.

Abner reflected on his life as he climbed; the times he'd run hungry and wild in the woods, the day Tabitha was born, living to watch over the young *maedel*, and then helping her with her scheme to marry. He glanced briefly at Matthew, and Abner swiped at his wet face. *I have an accountability here, ta do what's right, ta save Tabitha. . . . Help me,* Derr Herr. *. . . Help me. . . .* The prayer had hardly resonated in his mind when he felt a blinding pain in his left shoulder. He lost his balance for a moment, until Matthew caught his arm and steadied him.

"Everybody, down," Abner cried, trying to ignore the pulsing pain. He himself stayed upright despite his command until Matthew pulled him down bodily.

"How bad is it?" Matthew muttered near his ear.

"Just a scratch."

"Uh-huh. You've done your part, Abner. Now stay here and we'll finish this."

Abner wanted to protest but couldn't find the strength. He sagged further onto the slate and let himself slide for a few feet while the others passed him by. He knew he should listen to the cries to find cover but couldn't seem to move until Anke's soft voice came to him, as if from a dream, and he wondered vaguely if he was dying. . . .

"You must continue, my dear, with your delightful tale—though I find it hard to believe."

Tabitha wet her lips, knowing that she need only catch Elam's attention for a moment so he would be distracted from his vicious shooting. She had heard no cry after Elam had last shot, but something told her instinctively that someone had been struck by the bullet.

"*Jah*," she said, daring to move from the doorway of the shed to stand out closer to Elam in the rain. "But it is the truth, Elam. Matthew is a mail-order groom."

"Bah! The man will be groom no longer when he *kummes* into my line of fire."

Tabitha ran then to throw herself bodily against Elam. She had no illusion that she could stop him, but she might get hold of one of his guns . . . and to her amazement, the cold steel of a pistol met her fingertips. She pulled blindly at the metal, then stumbled to the muddy ground as Elam shook her off. She clutched the weapon in her shaking hands and forced out her words in a low tone as she got to her feet.

"Elam, my hands are very shaky. *Sei se gut*, put down your gun and kick it to me."

"You're *narrisch*, my dear. You don't know what you're doing."

"I do, Elam."

"She does, Elam," Matthew said in a hoarse voice from behind the other man.

Elam spun as Matthew tackled him. Tabitha heard the other gun discharge and ran toward the men. Matthew had soon subdued the bleeding Elam and dragged him to his feet.

Elam clutched his upper arm and sneered at Matthew. "You're a fool, Matthew King! You're not worthy of her."

Tabitha watched as Matthew looked at her and gave her a slow smile. "You know, Elam. I believe you're right. I'm not worthy of her."

She smiled back at him and wondered when he'd become the groom of her heart.

Anke tenderly lifted Abner's dusty head into her lap while Aenti Fern muttered about his shoulder.

"Lucky the bullet went straight through or else he might have bled to death by now."

Anke bent her head and carefully offered her hands to steady him as Aenti Fern tied off the bandage.

Abner looked up at her then, owl-eyed. "Anke . . . Matthew and Tabitha?"

She smiled down at him. "They've caught Elam Smucker. He had handguns like the *Englisch* do. Bishop Kore is here ta tell ya."

"*Jah*, Abner. All will be well, I think. Elam confessed to buying the guns illegally in Farwell on one of his mail treks. So, the *Englisch* can now deal with him."

Anke bent to kiss Abner's forehead, careless of the dust and the company. He smiled up at her and she felt her heart throb in her chest.

"Anke . . . will ya marry me?"

She gasped in surprise, then wet his face with tears of joy. "Ach, *jah*, Abner. *Jah*!"

Chapter Thirty-Nine

The next day was church meeting, and Tabitha had stayed up late talking with Matthew. Now, they both resolutely dressed and held hands as they hiked from atop the falls down to the Fisher barn.

Tabitha was nervous. She had barely had time to talk with her *daed*, and she wasn't sure if his loving hug was out of thankfulness for her being alive or in reconciliation after the shunning. Also, she had no idea how the community would respond to what she had to say, but Matthew seemed confident, so she lifted her chin a bit as they entered the large barn toward the end of the service.

Bishop Kore must have seen them, and Tabitha winced as the *auld* spiritual leader gave the community a bright smile. "Now, this is nice and right, I think. We've shunned two of our own, searched for them, and *Derr Herr* has brought them back into our midst. We will now hear their confessions."

Tabitha bit her bottom lip as she faced the rows of solemn faces. She saw her *fater* nod, and Anke wipe at a tear with her apron hem. Abner stood resolute at the back. Then Matthew began to speak. "We are grateful to all of you who helped us yesterday. The time we've spent away from the community has been a time of reflection and deep thought. And we want to say, up front, that what we've got to tell you all may not be what you expect, but it is nonetheless the truth."

She listened as he began to speak calmly.

"I confess before you all that, *jah*, I did know about my wife's wood carving and I appreciated her talent in this area. I also confess that I still don't understand fully what exactly is wrong with women doing woodworking. But I owe you all a much greater confession. When I came here to marry Tabitha Stolfus, my true motivation was to get an apprenticeship working with you, John Stolfus. I've apologized to my wife for my deception, but the reality is that now I must apologize to all of you. You welcomed me, gave me gifts, showed love and friendship to me, and all the while, I was lying to you—because my first reason for coming was about wood carving. I humbly ask for your forgiveness."

There was quiet in the barn as all eyes now switched to Tabitha. She thanked *Gott* in advance for giving her courage. "I must confess that I would be lying if I said that I'd never carve wood again. For some reason, *Derr Herr* has gifted my mind and my hands to—see things in the wood. But I want to bring no shame to my *fater*, and I know he greatly disapproves of my carving—"

"It is I who have brought shame to my own name and to my own *haus*, *dochder*."

Tabitha was amazed to see her *fater* rise to his feet. She listened in astonishment as his big voice echoed in the lofty barn.

"Some of you may know that it's been said that

Tabitha's mother, Miriam, died of the influenza when Tabitha was but a babe. That is a lie."

Tabitha heard the soft gasps of the church members, then glanced at her *fater* and found him suddenly clutching at his chest, his face suffused with color. He sagged to the barn floor and there was only the sound of his labored breathing, coming harshly through his lips.

Tabitha saw Abner push past the unmarried men, and she felt Matthew's touch on her arm as she flew to kneel down at her *fater*'s side.

"I . . . can't . . . breathe."

"It's all right," she said, taking his hand between her own.

Aenti Fern had made her way to the ailing man and quickly studied her patient.

"Get a blanket," she said. "He needs ta be carried to the hospital in Farwell. He's had a heart attack, but I think they might be able ta help him there."

Tabitha watched as a blanket was positioned beneath her *fater*; then Matthew and Abner and Big Jim and Asa Zook each took a corner of the fabric and made their way out of the Fisher barn. She ran to stay beside the makeshift gurney, praying that they would get to Farwell before it was too late to save her *daed*. . . .

Abner used his right arm and hand to keep John's weight balanced on the blanket. He saw Tabitha's hair *kumme* down as she kept pace beside the fast-moving men. He looked down into John's eyes every minute or so, grateful that he could still see life in the blue depths.

The two-mile trek overland was accomplished as

quickly as possible, and Abner wasted little time with explanations as he put his shoulder against the emergency room door of the hospital.

A nurse tried to wave them down, but Abner steered the men in the direction of the swinging doors, with Tabitha still right alongside.

"Here now—what's all this?" Dr. Carmen met them, then paused to put his stethoscope against John's chest. He listened for a moment and nodded. "Get him in here on the table. Move!"

Abner was relieved to lower the blanket to the hospital exam table. His left arm ached from the gunshot wound and he had a bad headache. Still, he lost no time in shooing Tabitha and the other men away.

"It's best for ya ta wait out here. Matthew—*kumme*—hold yer wife."

Then Abner closed his eyes and leaned his head back against the wall, thinking how much he wished that Anke was there.

Anke had joined in the prayers that Bishop Kore led for John but was grateful when she could head back home and wait for news. She was pacing rather aimlessly with a dishcloth in her hand when there was a rapid knock on the back door.

Anke went to open it and was both surprised and shocked to find Grace Fisher peering at her through the screen. The younger woman had a black eye and was holding shaking hands to her bleeding lip.

"Grace, *kumme* in. Praise *Gott* ya came here."

Anke asked no questions, just helped Grace to the

kitchen table and fetched a wet washcloth. Then she turned back to the cookstove and made a steaming cup of lavender tea and took it back to the table.

"*Danki*," Grace whispered.

"Are the *kinner* all right?" Anke asked after a few minutes.

"*Jah* . . . he doesn't hit them. I—I just wanted to compose myself before I *geh* back."

"Ya can stay as long as ya need."

"*Danki* again, Anke. I'm sorry to *kumme* after what happened to John . . . but I have a quilt square for you."

Anke stared at her blankly. "A quilt square. For me?"

Grace unfolded a piece of tissue paper from her apron pocket and withdrew a fine piece of appliquéd fabric. "I thought of how strong the mountains are here at Blackberry Falls—well, you can see."

Anke gently fingered the bright colors of the mountains captured in full fall foliage. "Grace, I don't know what ta say."

"Your eyes have already thanked me, Anke. Please use it at your next quilting. I—I'm not sure I will be able to come—something—might *kumme* up."

"Well," Anke said, bustling to hold back tears at the gift. "Let's take care of ya now. How about some ice for that swollen eye?"

"*Nee* . . . I better *geh* back. He was—drinking and—he'll probably be coming awake and need some help."

"Don't ya need help?" Anke asked softly.

Grace shook her head with a sad smile. "*Nee* . . . I'll be fine."

Anke went to open the back door for Grace and

touched her gently on the shoulder. "Ya *kumme* here anytime, Grace Fisher. Ya hear?"

Grace nodded, and Anke drew in a deep breath of sadness as she watched the younger woman walk away.

Matthew tenderly swiped his wife's hair from her beautiful eyes and bent to kiss her forehead. They had been moved by a friendly nurse to a private waiting room. But still, the hours passed slowly, and Matthew found little comfort in the television and plastic cups of instant coffee. Instead, he concentrated on braiding Tabitha's hair and securing it with a stray pin he found among the soft tangles.

She leaned against his shoulder and he wrapped his arms around her, loving the delicate weight of her bones and the scent of her hair. But her soft tears shook him and he was infinitely grateful when a doctor opened the door and asked in gentle tones for Tabitha King.

It was late, but the hospital in Farwell offered hospitality rooms for those whose relatives were in Intensive Care. Still, Abner was reluctant to leave the waiting room and kept a midnight vigil with Tabitha and Matthew.

"Your arm must pain you, Abner," Tabitha said, peering at him from her plastic chair. "Perhaps you should have a doctor—"

"I'm fine," Abner snapped. "Sorry, my *maedel*. My shoulder does hurt and I hate waiting. How was he when ya saw him?"

"In a bit of a bad way, I think." Tabitha smiled wanly.

The heavy wooden door of the waiting room was opened and the elderly doctor who had first seen John came in. "Well, he'll pull through all right, but he can't run a mill anymore. He must avoid strenuous activities, keep calm, and think about what he eats."

Abner guffawed. "Well, *gut* luck with those things, Doc. Though I bet he'll do the thinking about eating bit . . ."

"Well, it's up to you and his family and community to help with lowered stress. Now, he's asking for Abner?"

"That's me."

Abner followed the doctor deep into the recesses of the hospital, where lives hung in the balance: a blinking, tube-ridden place of contrasting dark and light. When he entered John's room, he found that it was like visiting a cave, and he wasn't prepared to see John as part of an ordered mess of monitors and equipment.

The doctor left and Abner slowly approached the bed. He took the hand that John held out to him. "Heart attack," John said hoarsely.

"*Jah*. . . . It's time ta mebbe slow down some."

"What of the mill?"

Abner gave his hand a hearty squeeze. "I believe ya already know that answer, John."

Chapter Forty

By unspoken agreement, there was no mention of the shunning when John came home from the hospital. Still, Matthew decided to *geh* talk with Bishop Kore while Tabitha was helping Anke in the kitchen one afternoon.

Matthew walked through the bare November trees, his boots breaking the frost on the ground. The sky was leaden, threatening an afternoon snow, and he thought about taking Tabitha for a sleigh ride if they got enough on the ground.

The walk to Bishop Kore's reminded Matthew of first coming to Blackberry Falls and of how much had changed in such a short time. He had thought that he had everything worked out the way it was supposed to *geh*, and *Gott* had showed him a very different but better plan.

He gained the steps of the bishop's small cabin and knocked briefly. The door was opened and Bishop Kore gave him a hearty welcome.

"Matthew, my *buwe*! What can I do for you? Perhaps some lemming in butterscotch. . . ."

Matthew took off his black hat and smiled at the *auld* man. "Why do you talk like that?"

"Because my role can be difficult and I need to have some humor to lighten things up at times."

"Wow," Matthew said, blinking at the lucidity of the response.

Bishop Kore laughed. "But don't let anyone in on the secret. They just think I'm *narrisch* except on Sundays."

"Okay, you have my word."

"But that's not why you've come, is it?"

"*Nee*. I wanted to talk to you about the shunning. I'm not sure where we are with that. Once John is well, should we move back up to the cabin above the falls?"

"In truth, I believe that *Gott* has a way of working things out. So, stay and help John for now."

"All right, if you say so."

"I do," Bishop Kore intoned, then gave him a broad wink that made Matthew laugh and set about the rest of the day with a light heart.

Anke crossed her arms over her chest and tapped out tense sounds with her right foot. "*Nee*," she said bluntly.

Tabitha gave her an exasperated sigh. "But why, Anke? Daed is on the mend and it'll be fun. After all, I didn't do it for my wedding and—"

Anke cut her off with an exclamation of triumph. "That's it! We will do it together, so it won't seem like I'm tryin' ta hog attention."

Tabitha laughed merrily and Anke couldn't hold back a smile herself at having solved the knotty problem of a wedding quilting.

"Sit down and have some tea," Anke suggested, and

she was pleased when the younger woman agreed. Anke looked at her former charge and found herself remembering Tabitha's usual reluctance to do work in the kitchen.

"You've grown into a fine young woman," Anke said softly.

She smiled as Tabitha reached out a hand to squeeze her arm.

"I would not have grown much without your teaching. *Danki*."

Anke felt herself blush at the praise, then spoke again. "I thought your ad for a mail-order groom was a wild scheme, I have ta admit. But Matthew is a *gut* man."

"And so is Abner," Tabitha said teasingly.

Once more, Anke felt herself flush, but there was *nee* denying the truth of what Tabitha said. She sighed softly. *Abner is a very* gut *man indeed.*

"Anke, I do believe that you are deeply in love and that is *wunderbaar!*"

"Sometimes I feel foolish," Anke admitted.

"Whatever for?"

"Ach, I'm no young duckling anymore."

"Ducklings are a dime a dozen. . . . Abner wants a well-feathered duck—er, hen!"

And Anke had to laugh out loud. . . .

Abner came in through the back door and caught Anke around the waist. He loved holding her and pressed her rosy cheek with a hearty kiss.

"Well, sweetheart, you've got yer wedding date—the second Thursday in December."

He enjoyed her soft cry of joy. "Ach, Abner . . . I don't know what ta say. It's all happenin' so fast."

"Not fast enough, if ya ask me!" He pulled her closer and kissed her mouth, feeling a shiver run down his spine at her response.

She slapped his broad shoulder and laughed. "Ye're a wicked man, Abner! But I love ya."

He kissed her again. "And I love thee. . . . Now, tell me when we're ta set up that quilting frame for yer weddin' quiltin'?"

"It's ta be a double quiltin'. Tabitha will celebrate with me."

"Then that means I'll take young Matthew ice fishin'!"

"All right, but see that it's by moonlight that ya fish and not with moonshine!"

"Ya needn't fear, Anke!"

And they laughed together aloud.

Tabitha knocked softly on her *daed*'s door and was bade to enter. He had been sent home to rest and recover, and today, Tabitha was glad to see that he was sitting at the window, watching cardinals at play near the bird feeder.

"How are you, Fater?"

"Well enough. I think of the saying, 'When a cardinal appears, an angel is near'."

Tabitha smiled and drew a rocking chair close to her *fater*'s knee. "You're in a thoughtful mood, Da."

"Well, when you have a brush with death, Tabby, it

makes everything in this world look different." He turned to give her a sad smile and she reached out to take his hand.

"Do you . . . want to talk now, Daed?"

She bit her bottom lip, wondering if her question was inopportune. She had tried not to ask about his words to the community right before his heart attack. . . . Now she hoped she wasn't pressing too hard.

But her *fater* seemed to welcome the chance to talk, for he turned to her eagerly. "I remember what I said, Tabby—right before my heart attack. I . . . meant to say more, of course, but now I'm seeing things in a different light, which I believe to be a change wrought by *Derr Herr*."

Tabitha found she was holding her breath and quietly exhaled. "What do you want to say?"

"I'm the reason your mother left Blackberry Falls. I chased her away. I was jealous, I suppose, of the gift *Derr Herr* gave her." He looked at Tabitha and nodded. "She was the best wood carver I've ever seen. But maybe, maybe you have the gift as well."

Tabitha swallowed hard. "I love to carve."

"And I had you shunned for that love. Just as, years ago, I used my influence on the mountain to convince a newly widowed Bishop Kore that women should not be permitted to carve wood."

She was appalled to see his eyes fill with tears. "Ach, *sei se gut* don't, Fater."

"*Nee*, these are *gut* tears. Tears of regret, *jah*, but tears also of rejoicing—rejoicing for you and Matthew, Abner and Anke, and your skill and craftsmanship."

She felt truly humbled by his words, but she had to ask. "What happened to my mother?"

"Ach, child. . . . I forced her to leave, to choose between wood carving and life here. Remember again, this was jealousy on my part. A great sin. She left our life behind, never to return, but she wanted me to promise to give you the ladle. You teethed on the beautiful thing."

"I have it still."

"I know." He cleared his throat. "The doctor said I've got to settle down, change my way of living. I can't run the mill anymore, Tabby." He caught her hand and drew her close. "But I've been thinking on it, and I know that, in other communities, Amisch women run their own businesses. Even here, Abigail runs the pottery." He smiled at her and there was confidence in his voice. "You can run the mill, Tabitha. You can do it."

She stared at him. "What—did you say?"

Chapter Forty-One

Thanksgiving flew by in a whirlwind of pumpkin spice, pudding and cake, braided raisin breads, and rich meats from the depths of the forest. The festivities didn't end with the holiday, though, as Tabitha and Anke's quilting was set for the following Saturday and a large quilting frame was assembled in the Stolfus living room.

No mention had been made yet that Tabitha was to run the mill, but the family rejoiced in the private knowledge. Still, John said that the men would need convincing to be led by a woman and that he was praying for the right way to tell them. In the meanwhile, though, Tabitha reveled in the preparations for the quilting and Anke and Abner's upcoming wedding.

The day finally came for the quilting and Anke insisted on making some of the food herself. So, the kitchen was piled with platters of delicate finger sandwiches—egg salad with olives, ham salad, cheese and pimento, and cucumber and chives. And the women of the community had plans to bring food as well. Outside, the first snowstorm of the season was making the woods into a fairyland.

Tabitha soon found herself sitting between Gross-muder Mildred and the only man at the event—her husband, Matthew.

"But you can't quilt," she'd sputtered when she'd first heard of his plan to stay.

"And why not?" he'd asked with a teasing smile on his handsome face.

"Because you're a—man." Tabitha realized the error in her thinking. If a woman could run a mill, then a man could surely quilt.

Matthew had kissed her soundly, and now she was grateful for his long legs brushing hers beneath the quilt as he sat beside her, quilting like a true craftsman.

"Ya say ya like ta quilt and sew, young Matthew," Grossmuder Mildred observed from her seat, where she deftly used her fingers rather than her eyes to produce tiny stitches with ease.

"I do. Learned from my *mamm*'s sister when my *daed* wasn't looking."

His remark set the women off into gales of laughter.

Later, though, when Tabitha's turn came to have a break and let another woman take her place, Matthew pulled her into the kitchen.

"What is it?" she asked, wondering at the dimple beside his mouth—a sign that he was up to some mischief.

"Wrap up warmly and put on Anke's boots. I have a theory I want to test out."

Bewildered, she did as he asked, and soon he was helping her through drifts of snow.

* * *

Anke shyly embraced her special day with quiet grace. It was difficult for her to be the center of attention, but Abner had made her promise that she would enjoy herself at the quilting and she discovered that she was having fun.

She was seated next to Abigail from the pottery on her left and Grace Fisher, who had *kumme*, after all, on her right. Anke concentrated on not asking Grace any personal questions and kept the talk light. She needn't have worried, for Grace seemed to be enjoying herself.

Abigail, though, spoke quietly. "Tabitha told me of John's wishes for the mill."

Anke was surprised but nodded.

"Please tell her and John that I think I have a plan to help convince the men."

"All right. *Danki*, Abigail."

Anke didn't want to ask any more questions lest someone overhear, so she accepted a piece of chocolate cake with fluffy peanut butter icing and took it into the kitchen to eat, far from the quilt top's bright, pretty surface.

She was surprised to see Abner stamp inside on the mat with his great boots and was about to put down her cake when his smile stopped her.

"Why aren't ya ice fishin', Abner?"

His blue eyes were warm. "Because I'm just in time for another treat, it appears."

"Ach, would you like—"

"*Jah*," he answered. "I'd like a bite of your cake, please."

"All right." She stepped near his big, snow-covered frame and lifted a forkful up to his lips. He ate it with every appearance of delight, then pulled her close to his cold chest.

"Chocolate cake with peanut butter icing." He laughed. "There's only one thing sweeter."

"What's that?" she asked, joining in his playfulness.

"You."

And he'd convinced her in moments.

"You're out of breath, sweetheart," Matthew teased as they finally reached their destination.

"Well, I was prepared for a quilting, not a hike, though I've learned to always be prepared for anything with you."

"*Danki*," he said, then *bussed* her soundly on the cheek.

"But why are we at the falls?"

"Because we have a long overdue date with some faerie singing."

He was pleased by her smile.

"You know that's just a legend, Matthew."

He shrugged. "We'll see."

He led her carefully across the slippery rocks and behind the icy spray of the falls.

"Now," he said, turning her to him and loosening her scarf. "Let's hear those faeries sing."

And they did.

The following Monday Abner stood with his arms crossed in front of the men at the mill. They'd gathered early as John had requested and were now asking about the security of their jobs if John was not well enough to run the mill.

"Jest hold on a minute," Abner said firmly, knowing that the mood of the men was rough.

He was relieved when John finally came out of his office with Tabitha holding his arm. Matthew moved among the men, handing things out.

Then John began to speak. He told the men the truth of how he'd lost Tabitha's mother because of his own stubbornness and unfairness. Then he patted Tabitha's arm. "*Geh* on, my dear."

Abner worried for her but had to admire her strong spirit as she stood in her long black cloak with her chin lifted. Then he listened with appreciation as she began to speak.

"Blackberry Falls and the forest run in our blood. All of our blood. My *fater* is not trying to make something right today, but to make something better, I pray. So, it is with pleasure and humility that I take over the running of Stolfus Lumber and Woodworking. It will be my privilege to serve as your leader."

Abner listened to the faint murmurings of the men gathered and waited. Then he spoke himself.

"Take a look at what ya hold in yer hands before ya open yer mouths in disapproval. Tabitha carved each one of those creatures you hold. She's given them to Abigail at the pottery these past years. And ya can recognize their workmanship."

Asa Zook spoke up. "These carvings are better than anything that's ever come from my hand. I got no problem with havin' Tabitha as my boss."

Abner was relieved, and soon the other men took up Asa's call and Abner was pleased to see the girl he'd protected for so long become the rightful leader of her family's business.

Epilogue

The delightful sounds of the celebration of Anke and Abner's wedding were muted below as Matthew led his wife to her old bedroom with a soft tread.

"Matthew, what are you thinking?"

He heard the warm love in her voice and kissed her for a moment before he eased the door closed behind them. "I'm thinking, *mei* sweet, of something very different from the hard wood of this floor against my back that I knew during *nachts* past."

He watched her smile thoughtfully, as if considering his words. "You want to test the softness of my girlhood bed?"

"*Jah*. As wicked as you've made that sound . . . *jah*."

She giggled. "*Jah*, it is."

But when she would have led him across the room, he stopped and caught her close, easing a flat stone from his pocket. "Do you remember this?" he asked.

"Our first wedding gift! The seashell fossils in the rock . . . I thought it had been somehow misplaced in the move."

"*Nee*. I've had it all along." He let his fingers rest on hers as she traced the outlines of the shells.

She lifted luminous blue eyes to meet his gaze. "Why?"

"Do you remember what the bishop said? About shells not belonging at the top of Blackberry Falls, but still being there just the same?"

She nodded and he smiled down at her. "I was like these shells, Tabitha. I belonged, but not really . . . not until I knew the truth of your love. You've given me so much, *mei frau*, and I want our lives together in Blackberry Falls to leave an imprint in time, one that our *kinner* and those beyond will see and remember as surely as we can see these shells."

She gently took the stone from him and leaned against his chest. "I love you, Matthew."

He heard her soft exclamation of surprise when he neatly scooped her up in his arms and began to walk toward the bed. "I love you too, sweet." He grinned when she deftly slid the first pin from his shirt, feeling his heart begin to thrum.

"*Gut* that we're married," she murmured.

"True." He gently lowered her to the soft bed and slid the fossil to a resting place on the extra pillow.

"Are you planning to create a lasting imprint of love in my memory, *mei* mail-order groom?"

Matthew swiped a kiss across her lips, then laughed. "*Jah*. I think I will. . . ."

And he did.

Still, he was unprepared for the brutal backhand his *fater* calmly delivered.

"Why did you do it?" His *fater*'s straight, yellowed teeth looked like an animal's, and Caleb struggled to focus for a moment as he licked blood from the side of his mouth.

"Every other suitor within a fifty-mile radius was at her *fater*'s funeral, but not you. Yet it's you Charity Miller wants, and I swear it's you she'll have."

Caleb resisted the urge to close his eyes against the memory of the last encounter he'd had with Charity Miller. He'd caught her kicking a stray dog with a well-shod foot, and when he'd picked up the animal and out of harm's way, the girl had merely shrugged at him with menacing eyes. "What difference does a stray *hund* make?" she'd sneered. "Besides, sometimes it feels *gut* to let others know who's in charge. Don't you think?"

Caleb had felt vaguely like throwing up or giving her a taste of her own medicine. He'd shuddered to think that his *daed* wanted a marriage between Charity and himself. A marriage to join their adjacent farmlands to create King's Acres—the largest farm in the whole of Clinton County.

Now Caleb snapped back to the moment and looked into his *fater*'s forbidding face. He squared his shoulders. "*Nee*, Fater. I will not marry Charity Miller. I have another . . . engagement."

"What? Where?" the older man bit out in red-faced fury.

Caleb smiled and clutched the newspaper tighter. "In a place called Blackberry Falls. . . ."

Please read on
for an excerpt from Kelly Long's
next Amish Mail-Order Grooms novel,

Courting Caleb.

Prologue

WANTED: An Amish Mail-Order Groom. Age 20–30. Must understand that courting will follow the marriage ceremony in *gut* order. Seeking one who is reserved, quiet, and bookish. Must cherish a woman as the vessel of *Gott*'s Making. Bride would prefer groom to write poetry and have a cultured reading voice. Reply to: Abigail Mast, Blackberry Falls. . . .

Twenty-five-year-old Caleb King read the ad from *Renova Record* for the fifth time, then shook his he̶ He eased back his black hat from his forehead and le̶ against the warm side of his horse, Tommy. He felt with the horse . . . *no questions . . . no demands. . .*

He glanced up as someone slid open the barn do̶ squinted in the sudden ray of sunshine from the̶ winter day. When Caleb turned and saw that it ̶ *fater*, he had the childish desire to hide the ne̶ behind his back and probably would have if the s̶ hadn't been so deadly serious.

Chapter One

It was a cold November afternoon as Abigail Mast, the local potter of Blackberry Falls, gently lifted a paintbrush and touched it to the dab of pink paint she'd made from juiced mulberries. She swirled the color onto the mug she held in her opposite hand and steadily shaped the first petal of a rose. The action was calming, and she needed peace—especially today. She shivered as a new gust of winter air blew in through the open door and swirled past her ankles. She liked to leave the door open to catch the sun even on the most intemperate of days.

"Abigail Mast?"

The mug fell from her hand and smashed on the hard-wood floor of her cabin. She glanced up to the open door-way and frowned at the stranger who stood there. Dressed in *Amisch* clothing, he was big and broad shouldered. The afternoon sun glinted on his overly long blond hair. *At least he has his hat in his hands,* she mused. *He isn't all that threatening. . . .* She was used to living alone on the fringe of the community and she preferred it that way.

"Who are you?" she asked, putting down her paint-brush. She bent to scoop up the pieces of fired clay and he quickly joined her, getting down on one knee.

"Here . . . let me help you." He tossed his hat onto the nearby table, narrowly missing the wet paints, and then set to picking up the remnants of the mug. She couldn't help but be aware of the fresh pine scent that clung to him and frowned at herself for even noticing.

"*Danki*," she said when he'd made a small pile of the pieces on the table. "Now, who are—"

He looked up at her with startling blue eyes framed by thick lashes. "I'm . . . the answer to your ad."

"My ad . . ."

He blinked, and she was once more struck by the unusually intense color of his eyes.

"*Jah*, the ad—for the *Amisch* mail-order groom. I'm it."

She rose to her feet, and he hastily got up off his knee. "But . . . I don't understand," she said.

"You did write the ad? I—thought I'd respond in person."

She gazed up into his handsome face and shook her head slightly. "But . . . he's already here."

"Who?"

"The *Amisch* mail-order groom. He arrived this morning. . . ."

Caleb felt a sinking in his stomach as he came to grips with the words she spoke. *Idiot . . . Of course another man is here already. I should have written. . . .*

"Where have you come from?" Abigail asked with a frown, as if searching for a way out of the dilemma.

"Renova," he said absently. "My *bruder*, Matthew, married someone from here a few months back."

"Ach, you mean my *gut* friend, Tabitha Stolfus."

He looked at her, taking in the sheen of her brown hair where it disappeared beneath her *kapp*. She was tall and held herself erect with perfect posture, yet the top of her head barely came to his chin.

"Does Matthew know that you're here?"

Caleb sighed to himself and shook his head. "*Nee*—I came rather suddenly."

"Well—" He watched her wet her lips. "I suppose—"

"Great walleyed catfish and pork bellies! Who do we have here?"

Caleb turned to see a spry, elderly *Amischer* with a thick, gray beard standing behind him.

"I'm Caleb King. . . . I came to see Abigail because—"

"Because, uh, he's Matthew King's *bruder*. He wondered if I knew the way to Tabitha and Matthew's," Abigail put in quickly.

Caleb turned back to watch as a flush stained the fine features of the woman before him. Clearly, lying didn't come easily to her, and the thought made him strangely glad. He wasn't about to betray her to the *auld* man.

"*Jah*, my *bruder*, Matthew . . ."

Caleb paused and Abigail hurried on. "Uh, *sei se gut*, excuse me, Caleb. This is Bishop Kore."

Caleb shook hands as he thought rapidly of the circumstances. *Lying to the bishop. It was enough to get a body shunned, but still, she risked it. Was it possible that she had not sought permission to write the ad?* "Bishop, sir, perhaps you would show me to my *bruder*'s. I've got my horse and dog out back here."

The bishop nodded. "MoonPies and Popsicles! Let's *geh*!"

Caleb resisted the urge to study Bishop Kore's bald pate, wondering what ailed the *auld* man, but then, Abigail Mast acted as if such talk was normal. Caleb followed the bishop out of the cabin and briefly turned back to look at her. *There's something about her that makes me think of swimming in deep water. . . .* But then he shook his head and walked out into the sunshine of the autumn day.

"I cannot believe that this has happened! Two of them! What are you going to do?" Mercy knew her voice had risen an octave as she stared at her younger sister. Abigail looked as serious and thoughtful as usual, and this only irritated Mercy more. She could never fully understand Abigail's calm yet closed personality.

"They say still water runs deep," Mercy muttered to herself. Then she straightened and glared at her sister once more. "Abigail—I'm serious. What are you going to do?"

"Perhaps marry Phillip Miller. He got here first. . . ."

Mercy put her hands on her hips, pinching her ample curves to calm her temper. "I don't know why you have to marry either one of them. What kind of thing is it to send in the mail for a husband? Your life is full enough at the pottery, isn't it? Why do you—"

Mercy stopped speaking abruptly as her fourteen-year-old *sohn*, Joshua, entered the cabin with a blast of cold air. Mercy sighed to herself as she considered her *buwe*'s tall frame and shock of wheat-colored hair. He was every inch his father, and Mercy had to admit to herself and to *Gott* that she wished Joshua resembled her instead of the shiftless *Englischer* she had thought loved her.

"I fed the chickens, Mamm. Can I head out to do some ice fishing now?"

Mercy frowned. "With Tad?"

Tad was a troublemaker if she'd ever seen one. The *buwe* had been in and out of mischief since the day he turned ten and rode Grossmuder Mildred's pet hog, Henrietta, through the cemetery and burial service of *auld* man Tucker.

"*Jah*," Joshua broke into her thoughts. "With Tad. Okay?"

She nodded reluctantly. "But be back by supper and make sure you've got a few trout to put on the table."

"Sure will, Mamm. *Danki*. Goodbye, Aenti Abigail."

Mercy watched her younger sister embrace Joshua and wondered for the fourth time how she was going to help Abigail out of her marriage mess.

"You don't need to worry about this, Mercy. I'll figure things out," Abigail said briskly once Joshua had closed the door behind him.

"How?"

"Well," Abigail mused, "*Gott* says that He is working things out for good in our lives if we love Him, so maybe there were always meant to be two mail-order grooms."

"You cannot marry two men!"

Abigail gave her a sudden smile. "*Nee*, but perhaps I can court two. I hadn't wanted the bishop to know about the ad, but now I think it will be all right. I'm going to talk with him this very minute."

"Court? Two? Wait! Let me *geh* with you."

Mercy snatched up her black cloak and followed Abigail outside, even as she muttered to herself about the burdens of being an *aulder* sister. . . .